OUT FOR BLOOD

Out for Blood

(Blood Rights, Book Seven)

K. B. Thorne

Love is underrated. This story—though not the grumpy parts of it—is dedicated to my family.

CHAPTER ONE

Being liked is highly overrated.

There are people—certain people, a very few people—who I love and would put myself in front of a train for. That does not, however, mean that I always *like* them, nor do I always want them to like me. Yet the world is obsessed with liking and being liked, and it's just fucking overrated. You know what comes with being liked? Work. That's what. And stress. And cooties.

Yes, I said it.

In case my cheerful demeanor hasn't given it away, my name is Dakota. I'm a bounty hunter that chases down the things that go bump in the night, or in the woods, or in the parking lot of the local supermarket. If there's a supernatural beast making a nuisance of itself, I'm the one that gets hired to hunt it down. Sometimes that 'beast' is humanoid, like a vampire. Sometimes it has four legs, twelve legs, I don't give a damn. Give me something to hunt and I'm gone. That's how it is, and that's how I like it.

But it seems for a while now, people have been trying to make me be...nice, and social, and likeable. God, I hate it.

Tonight was alright, though. I was hunting down a large wolf-like thing that had been raising havoc just outside of town—that town being Adelheid, Connecticut, which happened to be where I lived. That made for a short commute, and animal hunts tend to not be as crafty as humanoid ones, so it wasn't that hard. But I got to run around in the woods during a New England summer and no one bothered me, so I was content with that.

I stood in human form as I stared across the clearing at the thing. It was the size of a small horse and had ragged, spiky black fur jutting out at every conceivable angle, as well as a few inconceivable ones. The beast's eyes were not red, and acidic saliva wasn't dripping from its jaw or anything, before you ask. (Where do you humans get your ideas about this stuff?) It really was just a bigger, nastier wolf. It was kind of...generic preternatural, so nothing to get excited about.

It came running at me, and I lifted my arm, pulling the trigger on my tranquilizer dart gun. My dart caught it in the back of the neck. The beast growled at the sting, but kept running for a few moments. Once it was about four or five feet away from me, it started staggering like a drunk. I admired its tenacity as it continued to head in my direction, although I didn't give it the pleasure of trying to get away. It kept up its inelegant movement until it fell flat on its chest, unconscious, with its head on my foot.

Suddenly worried about acidic drool, I moved my sneaker away and took a look at it. No, we were good.

As handy as the tranquilizer gun is, there's one considerable drawback. I have yet to figure out how to make the damn animal jump into the back of my SUV *before* I shoot it unconscious. Fortunately for me, I'm preternatural *and* pretty damn strong, but hefting an inert sack of wolf wasn't high on my list of things to do.

Oh, there is a second drawback: people, like friends and family, get really annoyed when I use it on them.

I got the smelly thing—all three or four hundred pages of it—over my shoulder and started walking.

Then my phone rang. Or buzzed, really. I kept it on vibrate because the sound was annoying.

Holding the creature in place with one arm, I fished the

phone out of my pocket with the other and looked at it. It was my brother.

"Hi, Eddie," I said.

I heard the long moment of annoyed silence and then, "Don't call me that."

Smirking, I said, "Okay, Freddie."

"Shut up, woman!"

"What the hell are you calling me for?"

There was another long pause. "I don't know."

If I were in a comic book, a dot-dot-dot would have floated over my head. "You do remember that you called me just, like, eight seconds ago?"

"I know, but you annoyed me and now I've forgotten."

I made a face, despite the fact he couldn't see it. "Whatever, man," I muttered and hung up on him, stuffing the phone back in my pocket and starting to walk again.

Approximately ten steps later, my phone went off a second time. Sighing, I took it out and saw it was my brother, again. "Remember why you were calling?"

"Yes, smart-ass," he said. "Lorelei wanted to get your opinion on one of the pens and the shelter in the far back yard."

"Why didn't she call me herself?" I frowned. "She has my number, and I don't bite. Or, at least, I have no intentions of mauling her."

"She's still scared of you," he replied flatly, "and feels bad about using your money and your house to start all this."

I rolled my eyes.

Lorelei was my brother's girlfriend, who he had met while pretending to be a dog—I mentioned we were preternatural—and then she stuck around after learning that he was more than a bullmastiff. This was before Cameron's Law made all of us supernatural beasties legal, so the fact that she didn't run away screaming when she learned this and subsequently land in the loony bin is actually pretty remarkable.

"Tell her that I'm not going to hurt her and the money and land and what-the-fuck-ever is fine. I'll be home tonight and can help with anything else then."

"Thank you." This time, he hung up.

See? This was what happened when people like you.

I turned off the phone and started walking again, thinking that the distance between my car and the clearing had somehow managed to get longer on the walk back than it had been on the walk in. Then again, the 'walk in' had been me sniffing and tracking and trailing, so this part should have been a lot shorter...

My phone buzzed in my hand. I looked at it and saw it was Sadie—one of the few people in the world I call by their first name who I'm not related to. She is kind of my boss, kind of my friend. It's complicated.

"What?" I said.

"You're chipper today," she replied plainly. "I wanted your opinion on something for the wedding..."

Wedding, right. Sadie and Vance had already eloped, but this was the ceremony for friends and family. They liked me, so I was somehow involved. And she would. Not. Shut. Up.

I stared at the phone for a moment as she kept talking and then interrupted, "Sadie, what in the name of hell has gotten into that graveyard-addled brain of yours—" She's a vampire. "—to make you think I know a bloody fucking thing about weddings?"

There was a long pause. "Because you're older than dirt and know things?"

Her lack of being flapped by my attitude annoyed me even more and I hung up on her, although pressing a button on a smart phone has nothing on slamming a plastic receiver into its cradle. Sometimes, I miss the old days.

Had someone stolen my car? This walk was taking forever.

My phone buzzed again. I answered it without even looking. "I DON'T HAVE ANY ANSWERS!"

"...I take it you're not interested in donating to St. Jude's Children's Hospital today?" This was the tiny voice of a woman on the other end of the line.

It hadn't been Edward or Sadie, and I stopped walking, sighed, and hung my head. My own voice got a lot smaller then. "I already donate on an automatic monthly cycle," I said quietly.

"Oh, I'm sorry." She hung up.

I suppose that was one way to get on the No Solicitation list.

Finally reaching my car, I stuffed the phone in my back pocket and found my keys in another. My shoulder was starting to ache like hell. The preternatural thing gave me strength and stamina, but it did not stop sore and awkward.

Unlocking the back, I opened the hatch and dumped the animal in. I blew out a gust of breath and was just shutting it when the wind shifted, and I smelled something that stood out.

There was something rotting not far away.

Chances were that it was a forest animal that had died, or some asshole had decided to dump their trash, but there was something... peculiar about it that roused my curiosity. I made sure my truck was locked. I figured I had a little time before the tranquilizer wore off and my car became At Risk, so I lifted my head and inhaled deeply.

It's amazing what a change in the wind can do. My senses as a human aren't nearly as good as my animal forms, so I wasn't surprised that I had missed it on the way in, but I followed it fairly easily now that I was focusing on it.

I didn't have to go too far. My hopes that it was a deer or raccoon were quickly dashed by the sight of a bloody sneaker sticking out from under a bush. I knew there was no way that this person was alive with that smell coming off them, but I had to check. Taking another sniff of the air to make sure there weren't any threats around, I cautiously neared the bush and pulled back the branches.

The body was of a woman who had died from some sort of animal attack, that much was obvious. There was clear damage to the back of her skull, and something had bitten and pulled at her neck and chest. There wasn't enough throat for me to even look for a pulse, but no blood was pumping.

The sight of a corpse, even one as gruesome as this, did not bother me like it did most people. I had seen too much in my long life, but I was saddened. Okay, so I don't *like* people, but it doesn't mean I want to see corpses everywhere. I was sure someone was missing her, and they would never be the same once they got the news.

Letting the greenery fall back into place, I stepped back and pulled my phone out. I wondered if my beast had anything to do with this, but I didn't think so. The timing seemed wrong, and the injuries did too. As far as I knew, the thing hadn't killed or even attacked anyone before I got to it.

Before I dialed the station, I noticed prints in the warm, soft dirt. I lowered myself to look closer and saw the rather distinctive shape of an animal—like a dog, or cat, or bear. I wasn't as good with by-sight identifications, but I'd be sure to point it out to the cops. Yet there was something...odd.

Frowning, I stared at the prints and realized that the distance between steps were wrong. It looked like something with animals paws that...walked on two legs? That made me blink a few times. Something must have happened to the prints to make it look wrong, because I didn't know any creature could do that. At least none with such a consistent gait.

I stood and backed away, finally dialing the police station.

CHAPTER TWO

By the time the cops showed up, I was hanging out on the roof of my truck as a cougar. I didn't want to run the risk of damaging the scene by doing anything else, just in case they needed anything. I stayed outside so I could hear and keep anyone away from it. The black-and-white pulled up alongside my SUV.

"Hey there, Dakota," the uniformed office greeted as she got out. 'Hey' from her mouth sounded suspiciously like 'ayuh,' I thought, but maybe that was just because I knew she was a recent immigrant from Maine. It took a while for the 'ayuh' to get out of the system, I had learned. That accent could almost be as stubborn as one born in the Deep South, but neither were as insidious as the Bostonian.

"Officer Hardy," I greeted as I shifted back to human. It did please me that the woman, though human, took me in stride. Well, maybe not 'please,' but it did impress me. It usually took a while for people to get used to seeing a cougar lazing around and knowing it was me.

The passenger door opened and another uniformed woman stepped out. This one I also recognized, but I knew pretty much every cop in town, for better and for worse. "Officer Diaz," I greeted her as I hopped down. She was from New York, as in the city.

She nodded at me. "So, you found a body?"

"Ain't it just my fucking luck, right?" I replied. We knew one another well enough for them to not suspect me, which was nice. I'd hate to have to break out of jail again. That always pissed the cops off. "This way."

The walk to the body wasn't too far. I pointed to the sneaker when we got there.

"I didn't touch it, although I did look closer just to make sure there was no chance of her being alive. Then I called you. I'm not a professional, but it looks like an animal attack. There are pawprints too, though I think some are already obscured."

"Thanks for the information," Diaz said in her usual straightforward kind of way. "We appreciate you not touching the body, of course. Since you know that just means more paperwork for all of us." Her full lips curved up in a smile. She was an awfully pretty woman, I always thought, and found myself wishing—not for the first time—that she swung my way. Sadly, no dice.

"You know me too well, Diaz." I snorted. Not like I had the time or use for a relationship. Not that I was any good at them.

"The coroner should be here soon as well as some techs. We just happened to be close," Hardy said. "We can take your statement now so you can be on your way."

I nodded. "Well, I'm out here 'cause of the unconscious beast in the back of my car. I was on a hunt, and this is where I got it. After I had dumped them and shut the hatch, I caught the smell of the body and followed it here."

Diaz was peering through the foliage at the body. "Definitely looks like an animal mauled her," she commented, turning to me. "Do you think your beast could've done this?"

I thought it through for a second time. "I won't say it's impossible, but it's been moving around a lot. It's taken me a while to catch them. That body had to be here a little while to get that smell going, and my beast hasn't really been in this area that long. Plus, it hasn't attacked anyone else we know of. But…I won't swear to it not being them."

Hardy took all this down on her notepad. I heard the approach of other cars and knew that the rest of the necessary crowd was arriving.

"Anything else?" I asked. "I'd like to get the monster to lock-up before it wakes and destroys the interior of my car."

After a thorough examination of her notes, Hardy nodded. "You can go. We have your number if we need you."

I merely nodded, not replying that it would be in their best interests not to call me. I just turned and left, passing the others as I got back to my car and drove off.

☾○☽

On my way home, between the forest and the place where I had to drop my beast off, I discovered that said beast had a very fast metabolism. It worked the strong, magic-enhanced tranquilizer through its system and woke before I could reach my destination to get rid of it. Throwing itself against the meshed gate between us, it nearly sent my car careening off the road.

With some truly colorful language—we're not talking single words here, but whole phrases of expletives laced together into remarkable monologues of profanity—I drove the car over to the side of the road and punched on the flashers. Turning in my seat, I pulled the tranquilizer gun from the passenger side and pressed it against the gate. It tried to snap at the weapon, but I wasn't so stupid to put the thing inside for it to do so. I was kind enough to wait for it to shut its mouth and move its head so I could shoot it again. I had no interest in it choking on the damn dart. This fucker wasn't dying on my watch.

It roared and snapped, thrashing against the gate again as I watched with annoyance until it collapsed. The colorful string of words continued as I turned back to the wheel and started the car on the road again.

From there, I was able to get it dropped off. I was nice enough to warn them about its metabolism and told them to move fast. See? I was just being peachy that night.

After I got that sorted and received my 'receipt' for his hairy ass, which would let me get paid when I turned it in, I went home. I didn't really want to, but I did anyway. Didn't someone once say that being a grownup is doing things you don't want to? I figured that at four hundred years old, I'd run out of excuses to claim to be anything less than grownup. And so I went home.

Home used to be—just a couple of years ago—a studio apartment above a Chinese food restaurant where I got a discount on the rent by playing cat and catching mice. Now it was a nineteen-acre plot on the outskirts of town. It had one old, two-story farmhouse in the colonial style and fences... lots and lots and lots of fences. Inside these fences were sheds and dogs. Lots and lots and lots of dogs.

Why was I living in a zoo? My brother and his girlfriend.

Okay, quick history. My brother and I were separated for a long time. We reunited a few years ago and didn't want to be parted again 'cause we're pretty much all we have left. But to find me again, he left his girlfriend Lorelei in Alabama. He met her through an animal shelter—long story, but remember, bullmastiff—and she's huge into animals. I told him to move her ass up here, but she didn't want to leave her animals. That had been the only thing in the way. So, I was nice, and see what it got me. I offered to help them get a place here where she could set up a big dog rescue and bring up abandoned pups on the underground doggy railroad to live up north, where they're more likely to get adopted than put the sleep.

That wasn't nearly as quick as I meant it to be.

Anyways, she was there. The house was there. Many of

the dogs were there.

Several of them rushed at their fences to bark at me as I drove up the long driveway. I couldn't tell from the car if they were excited or protective, but I wasn't sure I cared. They were barking and it was loud, drilling into my head as if I had a screwdriver at my temple. I honestly prefer animals to people, but not that many dogs at one time. It was beyond my tolerance levels, although I'm the first person to admit that my tolerance has always been a limited threshold. Plus, I thought some of them could smell the cat on me, since I spend as much time as a cougar as I do as a human. Shockingly, they get weird about that.

There was a carport next to the house, but the two slots were already filled, so I parked beside it. I got out of the car and trudged into the house to the symphony of dogs barking. Once inside, I shut the door behind me and found it was no better in there. There were three yapping little ones bounding into the kitchen and jumping at my legs. I just stopped and stared at them, too tired to even be annoyed. They were just dogs, after all.

Lorelei came running into the kitchen behind them, shouting all their names in such rapid succession that I wouldn't be able to tell you even one of them.

"I'm sorry," she drawled apologetically, gathering them all up in what I had to acknowledge was a truly impressive maneuver to contain all three at once and get them out of the kitchen.

Rubbing the back of my neck, I dumped my wallet and keys in the bowl by the door. I kept the phone, although I didn't want to do that either.

A few minutes later, Lorelei came back in, sans dogs. "I'm so sorry about that," she said again.

I waved my hand. For some reason, I couldn't seem to vent my annoyance at her like I did with everyone else. I didn't understand why, but there was just something in my head that made me be nice to her. It was annoying as hell.

"Don't worry about it," I said. "Edward said you had a question you wanted to ask me?"

"Oh, no," she said, smiling faintly. "I've already gotten it figured out."

I arched a brow. "Are you sure? You're not just saying that because you're afraid to ask?"

The blush was hard to see on her dark skin, but I could tell she was blushing. "No, I promise," she said. "I got it sorted."

I wasn't sure I believed her, but I wasn't going to press. I just stared at her for a moment longer, to see if she cracked, but she didn't. She didn't stop looking embarrassed either, though.

Admittedly, my brother had good taste in women. She wasn't beautiful in your Hollywood typical way, but I thought that just added to her own beauty. It was like that for me and my last relationship. I hadn't told Edward that I found his girl attractive, of course, because hey, I didn't want him thinking I was going to be hitting on her with us all living together. That would just be rude and awkward.

"My brother around?" I asked.

"He's out in the back kennels," she replied. "I'm actually just about to go out myself."

I nodded and let her go, walking the rest of the way into the kitchen and starting to riffle through the cabinets and fridge. I needed food, but I wanted to get it before they both came back inside. I loved my brother, but I really didn't feel like being bothered any more for one night.

I took a half a loaf of Italian bread that we'd had for four days now and the four slices of cold, leftover roast beef. A can of warm soda completed my meal as I hurried off to my room, shutting the door. Apparently, one of the dogs had been in there at some point because I had to wipe their hair off my bed, but then I sat down and ate everything with my hands. I just didn't care.

The little yappers started up again, so I turned on the television. It didn't drown everything out, but it kind of took the edge off and let me focus on something other than the noise. I watched them talk about the economy, and some government types barked about Cameron's Law and the "evil preternatural scourge" that had descended upon "our America" and all that bullshit. It had been years since the law passed and they hadn't quieted down at all. In fact, I thought they were just getting louder.

There was another story about a medical-technical-type lab place—yes, I know my terminology—that had set up shop in town several months ago. It was called Pre-Tech, and it specialized in preternatural stuff. Sometimes, vampires and werewolves and all needed medical tending, and it was a booming business to learn how to handle that, and to make all sorts of things to accommodate our supernatural species. The old-world vampires who had been sitting on piles of gold all these years—sometimes literally and not figuratively—were investing in research and development.

Pre-Tech had been one of the earliest and was now one of the biggest—and apparently the newest place to house a dead body. Some employee had been found dead in what was being called a "lab experiment gone tragically wrong," but with no other details. It made me curious, but the story ended and moved onto the weather. I still couldn't figure out why they bothered since this was New England. The weather was going to shift and make the forecast change in two hours anyways. After weather was sports, and as soon as golf came up, I lost all interest and shut the thing off.

I didn't realize just how tired I was until I woke up three hours later with all the lights on, Tupperware containers on my bed, and my shoes still on my feet. I fixed all of those and went back to sleep…

...until my phone rang eleven minutes later. I glared at it while reading Vance Johnston's number. I answered the phone with a hiss.

"You're such a cheerful person," he drawled.

"Speak fast or lose your life just shy of your wedding," I growled.

He paused for a long moment, knowing I was serious. "Party is at ten tomorrow night. Meet us at Five. You're the best man. You have to be there."

Smart man that he was, he hung up before I could say anything. I threw the phone at the wall and went back to sleep.

CHAPTER THREE

My phone didn't ring again until a little after eleven the next morning. It took several rings for me to remember that I had thrown it into the wall after Vance's call. So, I slid off the corner of mattress like a weird snake and crawled to the far corner where it had landed.

Looking at the display through squinting eyes, I frowned because I didn't recognize the number. It wasn't unusual for that to happen; it meant either telemarketer or new client. I hoped for both in equal portions.

"Dakota."

"This is the hunter Dakota, yes?"

New client. They usually weren't so specific when they were calling to get my money. It was only when it was someone who might have to pay out money that they got particular. "Yes."

"My name is Sophie Wilson, and I work for Pre-Tech." That made my brows go up. "We were wondering if you might have available time to come into our Adelheid office today."

"Do you want to hire me for something?" Let it never be said that I'm not a straightforward kind of girl.

There was a pause. "We would prefer to discuss that in person," she replied, very politic sounding, then added, "but yes."

I smirked. "What time do you want to meet?"

☾○☽

By half past one, the perky-voiced bitch in my phone's map app had directed me to the Adelheid office of the now seemingly infamous Pre-Tech. It was planted in the middle of one of the area's many forests, looking like it had taken out as little of the surrounding trees as possible in the process, which was something I appreciated. The parking lot was small and mostly filled by what I assumed were employee vehicles, telling me that this place didn't keep a big staff and didn't get many visitors.

I found a spot and then headed inside...or to the door. It was locked, and I pressed a button attached to a speaker. A grumpy voice came through to me, sounding tinny, and asked what my business was. I told them my name, there was a buzz and a click, and I opened the door to go inside. This led me into a straight corridor with no visitors' desk, further reinforcing the fact that they didn't get *any* visitors.

So, I started walking. Before I got very far, there was a woman in a dark blue pantsuit who approached me with a polite smile. I stopped and waited for her to speak first.

"You must be Dakota."

Oh, this one was quick. Someone named Dakota had just buzzed in at the door of a building that got no visitors... I managed to not say it out loud. "Yes." That was impressive self-control for me, as you may have guessed.

She inclined her head. "I'm Sophie Wilson. If you'll follow me?"

I nodded and waited for her to turn before following her. In my dark jeans and black t-shirt, I knew that I was underdressed compared to her slick, put-together look...but I didn't really care, because they needed me. I didn't know what for, but they wouldn't have called otherwise, so they just had to deal with what I chose to wear.

We reached the end of the hall, entered the elevator, rose to the second story—which apparently was the top floor—and then I was brought into an office.

It was a downgraded version of your stereotypical executive corner office with a big desk and a few chairs on one side while a sofa sat in front of the large windows on the other. The room overlooked the scenic New England forest. I paused a moment to take in that sight from up here before looking back to the desk where another woman sat on the other side, this one older than Wilson. She had that gaunt 'I paid money to look like this' look to her, but she smiled politely at me.

"Thank you for coming," she said, waving at one of the seats in front of her. I moved toward it and heard the door behind me close. Wilson's scent began to fade and I knew that she had left, so I kept my attention on the other woman. "My name is Mary Hill, and I'm the director of this office."

I nodded. She already knew who I was, so I didn't waste time with an introduction. She seemed to be waiting for something but cleared her throat when I wasn't forthcoming with banal chatter and continued.

"We have a situation." I loved executive talk; it practically was another language. People don't call me when they *don't* have situations. "There was an animal in our lab, and it's escaped."

I nodded slowly. "Is this at all connected to your recently deceased employee?"

She arched a well-groomed brow. "Why do you ask?"

Cagey. "One and one frequently equals two," I replied simply. "An escaped animal and a dead person who worked in that lab…"

Hill's lips pursed for a second and no matter what she said next, I knew that I was right.

"Yes," she finally said, because she knew that I knew. It would be stupid to lie and would be an insult to me. I didn't like people, but I was good at reading them sometimes; I had to be.

"So the animal has been loose about two days?" I asked, reflecting on the news story about the body.

Her lips pursed again, and her eyes tightened. My own brows drew down as I stared hard at her. "Almost a week," she said.

That set my alert buttons off in several ways. "How is the dead employee connected, then?"

Looking down at her desk, she sorted some pictures that clearly didn't need sorting. "He was inside the perimeter but not in the building."

"So, the creature stayed in the area?"

"Or at least returned two nights ago."

I frowned. "Why am I just being called now?" Normally, big scaries got loose and I was called in a panic the moment they saw them. Although the panic annoyed me, the time line did not, because the sooner I got to it, the better I could do. A delay would make my job harder, and it was suspicious.

"We thought we could solve it in-house," she replied after a long pause.

"Did you at least alert animal control?" She nodded. "Is there anything special about the animal?" I asked next. Normally, I was only called in on the preternatural cases.

This time, she shook her head. "We were simply studying it."

"And what is it?" I asked next. I didn't like this woman an. I didn't get a great feeling from her, but then, I often didn't from these executive types. They were usually too uptight and too concerned with stupid shit for my taste, and the stupid shit they were usually uptight about was stuff that made my work harder...and then they expected miracles from me to fix it.

"A jaguar," she said curtly.

I frowned. When you thought of lab animals, you thought of rats or monkeys, not big cats. "Why did you have a jaguar?" I asked bluntly.

She met my gaze. "They are magnificent animals." She spoke with an admiration I understood. "You must know what this company is, Ms. Dakota. We study matters related to the preternatural, and we are studying the DNA structure of the werejaguar and comparing it to the DNA of a pure jaguar."

I wasn't sure I saw the point since other companies had already done that, but I wasn't going to argue a scientific issue. It wasn't my area. I just nodded instead. Why couldn't regular animal control, or whatever their 'in-house' solution was, catch a plain old jaguar in the middle of a Connecticut forest? It wasn't like it wouldn't stand out.

Something didn't sit right with me, but even if there was something bigger going on that they didn't want to fess up to, no one was more qualified than me to handle it.

"Is there anything else I should know?" I asked, giving her an 'out' in my terminology just to keep her from squirming so hard she hurt something.

"It's female," she said. "Large for the species."

I waited to see if there was anything else, but when there wasn't, I said, "You know I don't work free, right?"

Hill smiled tightly and opened a drawer in her desk, pulling out a check that she slid across the wooden desktop to me like she was offering a bribe. I took it, looked at it, and nodded. It was a considerable down payment. "The rest after," I said simply, and she nodded. I stuffed it into my pocket and got to my feet. "I'll start around the building. I'll call when it's caught."

Without waiting for anything else, I turned and left.

☾O☽

Once I had gotten outside, without any signs of any other people, I pulled out my phone and called the local police department. It was the middle of the day so I didn't talk to anyone I knew, but I left a message for Vance about my new job and that animal control was aware, but now I was on top of it. (A later call couldn't tell me much about the Pre-Tech employee, just confirmed 'animal attack.')

Stuffing the phone back into my pocket, I looked around. I didn't see anyone standing about, just the cars in the parking lot and the building behind me. I shook myself for a moment and then shifted into my ever-favorite form. Not only did I prefer it, but why not use a cat to find a cat?

Unlike almost every other kind of shapeshifter, my magic is different. No one understands it, because it remains outside of what we've managed to comprehend scientifically. Every preternatural species that has come forward and made itself known to man has now been studied, both during legalizations and after Cameron's Law, but there's still this fuzzy gray area where biologists and zoologists and anyone else you can think of just throw their hands in the air and say "Magic!"

I'm the fuzzy gray area. I can change my body into other human forms and animal forms, so long as I have some personal knowledge of them. I can do it instantly, without the bone-cracking and tendon-snapping of the lycanthrope species, and—this is my favorite—I don't shred my clothing when I do it like they do. Everything inanimate that touches my body when I shift is incorporated into the "Magic!" that does the change.

Nice, right? The werewolves are so jealous.

I inhaled deeply and enjoyed the scent of summer around me, then I settled myself into moving around the building and taking in the scents I found. There were the trails of many, many different people, and I tried to sort them out. It wasn't that I needed to know about any of them, but I tried to make sure I didn't miss anything. Cats smell very different than humans, however, so I felt pretty safe in making sure I would find the scent.

It was at the backside of the building, opposite to where I had entered it, and it was distinctive from the rest, although not as much as I'd have expected. There was something almost…diluted in the scent, but it was hard to describe. Too many people crossing over a trail can obscure it, after all, which was undoubtedly what had happened. Still, it was something, and it was distinct.

I followed it into the trees, but it came and went and remained diluted wherever I followed it.

Once I was a little further from the building, I realized there was a second scent that was entwined around it. Like…something had been following it, or it was following something? Maybe it was after something, or maybe this was the employee it had killed. It was hard to say, except that the scent wasn't quite human nor animal. I couldn't tell what it was.

Near one cluster of trees, I came upon the very pronounced scent of blood. I knew this was where the employee—I couldn't even remember if it was a man or woman—had been attacked and, with this much blood, had undoubtedly died. I felt compelled to stop there. Not that death tended to have a strong impact on me, but something about the amount of blood put me off.

After that moment, I kept moving.

It was more of the same. I wove around the building in a spiral, pushing the circle as I moved outward from Pre-Tech. There was the jaguar's scent, diluted and inconsistent, and then the 'other scent' frequently overlapping it. It was more than a little annoying since the inconsistency didn't give me a good track, and the overlapping scent was indecipherable contamination.

Eventually, I called it good for the moment. I'd come back for a second round, but I had a little 'opposition research' to do...

Chapter Four

As soon as I morphed back to human next to my car, my phone was ringing. I almost turned back so I didn't have to hear it and let the "Magic!" just keep the sound stifled.

I answered it.

"Hey, sis," Edward said. I tried to not roll my eyes. "I need a favor."

"Oh yes, please, tell me what I can do for you," I drawled with minimal effort to hide my annoyance.

He paused. I knew he could read my tone, but he apparently elected to ignore it. "We have a dog that had to be left overnight at the vet. Can you pick him up and bring him back to the house?"

My brows knit. "Edward, you know the dogs don't like me that much," I replied. "I think it's the cat or something, but they get weird around me." I shrugged uncomfortably, somehow putting myself in mind of the dogs who were unsettled by me but didn't understand why. Or maybe it was just me. Edward liked to be a bear and they didn't see so bothered by him...

"It's not that bad," he said. "And this is one of the easy ones."

"There's a million of them at the house now, please narrow it down," I grumbled. "Why can't you guys get him?"

"We're just tied up, and you're already out," he returned. "It's Buster, the shy Pit-mix with the black patch around his eye."

I tried to think of what dog this was, and thought maybe I had an idea, but as mentioned, I didn't spend all that much time around the dogs. I supplied house and considerable funds, but the actual handling of the dogs went to Edward and Lorelei.

With a sigh, I said, "Fine." Then I hung up without saying anything else.

I got into the car and drove from Pre-Tech to the town's veterinary office. It was a booming practice run better than most human hospitals, with a staff of ten vets every day (seven days a week) and full on-call hours with emergency services. You had to be impressed at that.

I walked into the front office and a little yappy canine next to the door immediately started yelping. I gave it and its owner, an old woman with a pinched face, a glare. They both glared back and we all went about our own business.

I gave them Lorelei's name and phone number, as I had already forgotten what the dog's name was. I was told to go around to the other counter and wait for discharge, which I did.

Settling myself into the corner, away from everyone else, I pulled my phone out of my pocket and opened the browser. A quick search pulled up the Wikipedia article on jaguars, because who doesn't need Wikipedia?

So, the fun facts:

1. The only big cat native to the Americas.

2. Third biggest there is, behind lions and tigers.

3. Apex predator, like most big cats. Means it's at the top of the food chain.

4. Likes to swim.

5. Solitary, prefers stalking and ambushing. (I could relate.) Can climb.

6. It has an extremely strong bite, which allows it to pierce through armored animals. (This next part made me sit up a little straighter.) It is known to bite straight through the skull of its prey and pierce the brain. (I thought back to the body in the forest the day before.) Not unheard of to bite throat and suffocate, too. (Again, the body.) Dragging its prey into a secluded area to eat, starting at neck and chest. (Again...body... All the blood at Pre-Tech in the brush.)

7. Compact and muscular, usually between 130 and 210 lbs. Some males recorded up to 350, with females being smaller. (The lady had said this was larger than average for the species, so I was guessing around 200.)

8. Territorial. Marks in the usual ways.

9. Crepuscular, which means active at dusk and dawn, though can be active during day or night and, unlike your common house cat, is active more than half the time.

The article did note that they rarely attack humans, and this one had seemingly already attacked and killed two...but then she wasn't in her natural habitat or any situation she could understand, so she was pissed. And who knew what else they may have done, poking and prodding her, at Pre-Tech? She was probably one really unhappy kitty and knew very well that it was the humans that had made her that way.

Oh, wonderful.

Jaguars were a protected species, so I had to wonder what legal machinations Pre-Tech had done, what acrobatics they had performed, to get that cat into their lab. Maybe they had made some kind of promises in their treatment and would release her into a sanctuary when they were done, but this whole 'hey, there are vampires' thing over the past few years had made some areas a little murkier than they used to be...

Either way, I had to catch the cat before she killed

anyone else. If they proved she had killed at least one of the victims, she was likely to be put down. I couldn't afford to worry about that, though, because that part wasn't my job… but my conscience (yes, I have one) was getting tweaked all the same, feeling bad for this cat.

Before I could wallow too deeply in that, Buster's name was called and I looked up. A small dog with the classic square Pitbull head was led out. He wasn't painfully timid but was definitely low on energy. They walked him over to me, and he paused, eying me with that 'who are you' look I had gotten to know very well. Unlike most of the other dogs I'd encountered, he seemed to be almost okay with me.

His head dropped, but the whip tail started wagging as he walked over and leaned that hard head against my knee.

I absently took the leash, but I was eying the dog in shock. None of the dogs reacted to me like this. Some were just the hyperactive type that rushed to and over everyone, but they didn't linger. The others just eyed me and sidled away. This one almost acted like…he liked me, but there was something in the hanging head that suggested he was asking me…

Like he was asking me not to hurt him.

That forced me to swallow hard and pet the dog's head. I sniffed, because I didn't cry, and looked up at the vet tech patiently waiting on me. She gave me a prescription bottle of pills that was a prettier color than they give to humans and a few pieces of paper with all pertinent information, which I took with a nod.

The woman behind the counter told me that the bill was taken care of, so all I had to do was take the dog home.

Buster sat in the front seat with me. Somehow, I couldn't bear to put him behind the gate like he was one of my captured critters. He was perhaps the best passenger I'd ever had, sitting still and not talking all the time.

I may or may not have asked Lorelei if there was any reason Buster couldn't stay with me. She may or may not have said that he could, and that she'd rather see him in a quieter place with a full-time person. I may or may not have been a complete and total sucker for that thirty-second moment in the vet's office and decided that Buster was my guy.

I'll never tell. Neither will he.

Chapter Five

After dark, I was sitting in my room. I kind of lived there to get away from the noise and the people, even if they were family, so I was on the bed leaning back against the wall. Buster's head was resting on my thigh. (Don't say it.) I thought he was asleep. I called the police department and this time was able to talk to Vance, because it was after dark so the vampires were awake and off to their nine-to-five (which has a whole new meaning when you're nocturnal) jobs.

"You're not calling to yell at me, are you?" he asked.

"No, why would I yell at you?" I was honestly confused.

He paused. "No reason. What's up?"

My curiosity suggested that I pursue why I should yell at him, but I decided not to. "Do you know anything about the body I called in last night?"

"I know that it's a body you found and called in last night..."

My withering look was entirely lost on him over the phone. "Anything else?"

I heard some papers shifting around and the clicking of a keyboard. "Not much. They're saying it's an animal, nothing native to the area so maybe murder by shapeshifter..."

This was where I told him about my new job and learned that whoever took messages during the day shift sucked. So I told him and let him know that while animal control was on the job, so was I, and that I thought there might be a connection. He agreed there might be, and I agreed that I would keep him informed. I think he was hoping for a rogue animal, because murder was more paperwork.

I pulled up a local map on my phone and looked at the place I found the body and then where Pre-Tech was. It wasn't impossible, but it didn't necessarily make sense for the cat to have killed a body there... The distance was mostly forest, but it wasn't right next door. If the cat had gone back to Pre-Tech, I would have assumed she had stayed closer.

That was when I looked at the time and remembered the bachelor party was that night. Vance was at work...

Right, that was why he thought I'd yell at him. Like I'd care that much.

I still had an hour, though.

"Want to go for a ride?"

Buster perked up.

☾○☽

We went back to where I'd found the body the day before. The immediate area was still marked off, but not too far out. It wasn't too hot a night, so I left the windows a little open and then went out to look around. Kitty form picked up the scent of cat, now that I was looking for it.

It was all still so diluted. Too many cops tromping around, I guessed. I kept looking and didn't find any of the usual territorial markers from your average big cat, yet as I moved, I did see large claw marks on some of the trees that I hadn't noticed before. A cat had been there and done some things to mark its territory, just not *all* of the usual signs...

The whole walk-around took about fifteen minutes, then I was back in the car. Buster greeted me with that dumb-ass grin and no apparent fear for the scent of cat that lingered around me, and I tried to figure out why that didn't bother him. I stared at him. He grinned at me. I took him back to the house and then went to the office for a quick check-in before the evening of forced socialization to follow.

☾O☽

"Please."

"Madison, I don't even know this guy."

"But you've met him."

"Once…for, maybe, five minutes."

"Vance likes him."

"And this affects me, how?"

Stopping in at the office had not proven to be my best move.

'The office' was the Stanton Agency, where I actually have an office that I occasionally can be found in but usually only when hiding from my brother. Or my house, these days. I hadn't been in the door for more than thirty seconds before Madison, the secretary and practically Sadie's sister, was onto me about her boyfriend and the bachelor party I was shortly due at.

All blonde and chipper, I never really knew what to do with her. Aside from work, we had virtually nothing in common. Still, she was a good person and always nice to me, if sarcastic at times, but I was okay with that.

"Chance is a fun guy, and he'll probably pay for the drinks," Madison said with a grin.

"See," I replied, waving a finger at her, "you say that now, but we go in and drink it up and he doesn't pay, I'm out a lot of money and will want someone's skin to compensate."

She couldn't resist a shudder because she knew I was just as likely to do it as not.

"Please?" She returned to her first tactic, actually sticking out her bottom lip and making her blue eyes bigger.

I winced. "Fine. Tell him to meet us at Five. I'm out of here before you find other people I have to invite to this forced social gathering."

She grinned and leaned over the desk, kissing my cheek. I shoved her off as she giggled.

See? Cooties.

Making my escape from the office, I headed to the outskirts of town where a bar called 5 had been built into an old Victorian. The upstairs was the 'living' area of the owner. I say 'living' because the owner is a vampire, so 'living' doesn't really take place. You know? The thing is, I don't think 'deading' is actually a verb. Nor is 'undeading' or 'unliving,' so I just have to go with 'living.'

Anyways, he owns a vampire bar. Usually, the only time I went there was on business, but what with my boss and her husband both being vampires, and the owner being a pretty cool vampire himself, it was the chosen spot for the night's festivities.

Aside from the last-minute addition, everyone was already there when I arrived. They had secluded themselves in a back corner, and I had to walk through the pungent smell of blood (vampire bar, remember) to get to them.

"How is it you're the last one here? Even your brother was here before you," Vance said as soon as he saw me, which was sooner than almost everyone else since vampires kind of rule the darkness. "You're my fucking best man and you're here last!" He didn't really sound upset, but I knew there was no way I was getting out of being harassed for showing up late. I should have had a go at him for having been at work earlier, but I thought it'd be poor form.

"She's not the *last* one here," a deep voice behind me said.

I actually jumped as I spun around, very not used to anyone sneaking up on me. Then I had to look up, because Chance Landry was taller than me. Being a shapeshifter, I get my pick of forms, and because I like to intimidate people, I keep myself usually around 6', but Madison's weretiger professional boxer boyfriend was 6'5" and broad—a preternatural heavyweight. He smirked at me and then around me to look at Vance.

"Madison talked her into letting me come along," he explained to the sort-of groom. (Since he was already technically married but having the ceremony now, I didn't really know what to call him.) "She wants us all to get to know one another better."

"You're perfectly welcome," Vance said, waving at an empty chair. "I don't know why she asked Dakota instead of me. She would've had to beg less with me." He grinned, flashing his fangs in my direction.

"Wrong place, wrong time," I muttered, taking the remaining chair.

Thankfully for my anti-social tendencies, the actual number of celebrants were few:

Vance, obviously, since it was his night.

Myself, of course. And my brother, smirking at my tardiness from the corner.

Then there was Daniel, a telekinetic human that Vance met during a...bad period, shall we say; Jackson, one of the pair of FBI agents assigned as the preternatural arm of the New London office, and a pyrokinetic; D, another vampire who works at the Stanton Agency; and then Sam, Vance's detective partner, a human with the ability of psychometry, and my ex.

Fun, fun.

We had, of course, seen one another since we'd broken up. When we'd been together, she lived in Hartford and worked there. But then chose to transfer to Adelheid when the job opened up, even though we had already split. This was the first time I'd had to spend any real amount of time with her in any sort of social capacity. I had been dreading it since I learned about it, because I knew as Vance's partner, she'd be here rather than with the bride's group.

I still wasn't entirely sure why we had broken up, really. Other than I'm a horrible person and why would anyone really want to date me…

There were already five open bottles of liquor on the table when I sat down.

"Watch your head," Daniel said. I blinked and saw his hand up, so I leaned to one side and watched as a bottle of tequila floated into his grip. He flashed a grin at me from behind his dark beard. I had only met him a couple of times, but he seemed okay. Usually, I do like to call people by their last names but no one had ever told me his and quite frankly, I was too lazy to dig it up.

"I'd toast to your last night of freedom, man," D began, smirking, "but it being too late and all…"

"Don't let Cassandra hear you say that." The amused rumble of thunder came from behind us. I wasn't startled this time, but I still hadn't seen him coming. *What the fuck, guys?* This was Quintus, a 6'6" vampire as dark as night and about as wide as a barn. He put a plate of food—sloppy chicken wings, BBQ spare ribs, quesadillas, and what-not—on the table.

I looked at the plate and then up at him. "Where the hell did you get food?"

Fortunately, it wasn't hard to get my meaning. "I picked it up special for the occasion," he rumbled with a grin, the whites of his teeth showing in the dark. "Just because I don't eat food don't mean I can't make it, and this is a special night. Just don't get used to it." He laughed—a sound like rocks jumbling together—before he turned and left.

Vance and D didn't eat, but the rest of us did. It was proper, messy bar food, and we were none of us too proud to not make fast work of it. I don't know where Quintus had gotten it, but it was good.

"Freedom is overrated," Vance declared, drinking from his cup filled with blood. B-positive cocktail?

I looked up at him and then around the table. Everyone but Sam and I—and I was just assuming this about Sam because I didn't like imagining the alternatives—were paired up. D had his vampire girlfriend, a sweet woman but very odd. Daniel had his teleporter. Jackson was dating Vance's former partner Nykk. Edward had Lorelei. And of course, Chance was dating Madison, although they weren't exactly 'exclusive,' as I understood. Not that I asked, of course, but I heard things. Chance moved around a lot with his career, so they were kind of more like 'when we're in the area, we're together' types. But he had come to Connecticut to go to the wedding/ceremony with her, which was nice of him, I thought.

Not that I spent a lot of time thinking about these things... God, what was happening to me?

"Well, if we can't lament the ball and chain," Daniel said, pouring another shot, "then are we supposed to toast to your long life of happiness together?" He chuckled. "Except you're both vampires, so...to forever without finding ways it's actually possible to kill one another?"

"Here's to an eternity of not staking one another," I offered.

"To a happily ever forever without lighting one another on fire," Sam chimed in. I smiled at her before I realized what I was doing and stopped.

"To near-immortality with anyone investing in vats of acid," Edward offered, and everyone laughed, making the 'oh' face that people make when something is so wrong but so funny.

"To a vampiric lifetime without putting secret sunroofs in each other's coffins." D gave a fang-filled grin.

Vance was laughing as he held up his hands. "Enough! Thank you, all, so much for your love and well wishes."

I poured a shot of werewolf whiskey. "You didn't expect this to be too sappy an occasion, I hope," I said, knocking it back and feeling like I was about to breathe fire. "That's for the ladies."

"Hey!" Sam exclaimed.

"She said 'ladies,'" Vance pointed out.

Sam laughed. "Oh, right."

"Still don't know why you chose me as best man," I muttered.

"Well," he said, reaching across the table to pour me another shot. "You're probably the most masculine person I know." He lifted his blood, and I lifted my whiskey. We toasted, downed it, and all worked the rest of the night on getting as drunk as we possibly could. We also made as much fun of Vance as we could. Even made a game out of it: one shot for every good snipe. It was fortunate for us that the vampires couldn't actually get drunk on blood, so they would make sure that we all got home before dawn to our respective hangovers.

Sam won. Or lost, depending on how you looked at it.

And Chance did pay the tab. By the end of the night, he might damn well have been my best friend.

Chapter Six

Late-morning light poured through the windows and had about the same effect as ice water as it splashed on my face. I stirred with a very annoyed groan but quickly learned that I could not easily move my legs. Forcing my eyes open, I saw that I was not alone... I wasn't even in my bed. Edward and I were a tangle of limbs on the living room floor, and Buster was curled up next to me.

He was snoring in my ear.

The dog, not my brother. Edward was snoring at my feet.

Pushing at my brother's face with the toe of my sock, I tried to untangle myself without waking either of them. Buster woke and licked me. Edward muttered something that sounded vaguely obscene, but I ignored it.

I stood up and immediately regretted it. Looking down, I couldn't believe that we hadn't even made it onto the couch. Hell, how had we even made it into the house? It takes a lot to get a preternatural drunk, but when we do... Wow. I realized after a moment that I hadn't even managed to stay standing and was, in fact, sitting on the couch now.

"How'd that happen..." I murmured, pushing myself back to my unsteady feet. Buster's dark eyes watched me with gentle concern as I steadied myself against the wall, feeling a terrible throbbing in both temples. "Don't ever let me do this again, guy," I said to him as we made our way into the kitchen.

The coffeemaker had already been turned on, and the pot was half-full on the warmer. I grabbed a mug without even bothering to check if it was actually clean and filled it. I drank half of it, fairly scalding hot, without leaving the counter.

"About time you woke up," Lorelei said in a more clipped tone than I ever could recall her using before as she walked in from outside. I knew she wasn't talking that loudly, but her volume was still too high for my pounding head.

"Quietly," I managed to say, pressing my fingers to the bridge of my nose.

"I can't believe how trashed you two got," she was sputtering and not any more quietly than she'd been talking before. Maybe she hadn't heard me? I didn't say it again, though, because I was likely to add some very unkind words and really didn't need to start some kind of brawl in the kitchen. I just groaned softly and drank the second half of my coffee. "I couldn't even wake either of you up this morning from where you were sprawled out like dirty laundry on the floor."

I grunted softly and refilled my cup. "Did you try?"

She spun around at me. "Of course I tried!"

Wincing, I clutched my temples and forehead with one hand and felt a growl rumbling low in my throat that I swallowed.

"I had to do all the morning work myself!" She was still talking. Why the fuck was she still talking? Did she not realize she was coming closer to being maimed, at best? "All that damn work should have been done already, except I was doing it by myself because you two were too drunk to even wake up."

I kept my eyes closed, because I knew that if I looked at her, I would tear her face off.

Was she actually standing there *admonishing* me? I had

given up a very, very large chunk of my savings to buy this property and set this all up so that my brother's girlfriend—not even *my* girlfriend! —could set up her dream. I gave money, I gave up my peace and quiet and privacy, and I had given a lot of my work to help get this rolling... I spend one night getting trashed at a friend's bachelor party and come home to get *chastised*?

Venom was rising in my throat, but I swallowed it down. It took a great deal of effort, and I felt a tremble starting in the muscles of my hands before moving its way up my arms.

"Aren't you even going to say anything?" she snapped.

"No," I said tightly.

My answer clearly surprised her. She huffed for a moment and then stormed out of the room, probably to go yell at my brother.

I looked down at Buster, who stared up at me uncertainly. I sat on the floor in front of the sink, and he sat next to me, licking my face. I let him.

"This is what you get for being nice to people," I muttered.

He licked me again, and I scratched his ears.

Animals are better than people.

☾O☽

I fed Buster breakfast but chose to not eat any myself. Just the idea of eating made me nauseous, but I let him eat. Then we went out for a run. I usually liked to run in animal form, but for him, I stayed human. He seemed to enjoy it, and I only had to call him back from squirrel-chasing twice.

After that, I dropped him back off at the house. He went straight to my room and jumped on the bed. I let him. I left the bedroom door open so he could wander the house—

if Lorelei had a problem with that, she could shut him in because I'd put a bowl of water in there—and then I went back to the site of the body I'd found. I wasn't sure why, but even my run hadn't totally cleared my head, so I figured, what the hell.

It only took a few moments before I was glad I had returned, because there was something different there today.

The immediate area was still cordoned off, but the kitty scent trails I'd picked up on before now had something else added to it. There was that weird scent I'd caught at Pre-Tech. It was fresher than it had been at Pre-Tech, and thus stronger. Not that being stronger helped me any, because I still didn't know what the hell I was tracking. All I knew was that it was there and hadn't been before, so someone or something that had been at Pre-Tech had now been here too...and only since yesterday.

Instead of focusing on the fading cat scent, I followed this new one. It wound around a bit strangely, but it did seem to be following the trail of the big kitty the same as I was.

The scent was so fresh, I felt like I might choke on it. What the hell was this thing? It had an almost human feel to it, but not really... Sniff... Sniff... The trail was really recent. So recent that it led right up to...

...a pair of boots.

I lifted my cougar head and followed the line of a pair of long, masculine legs, wondering how the fuck I hadn't noticed that there was another humanoid form here. I blamed the hangover; it was my only excuse.

Instantly backing up, I hunkered down defensively. I looked up the body and saw that he looked like a man, but he didn't smell like one. He smelled...like nothing I'd ever smelled before, and after four hundred years, that's saying something. He didn't look like he was about to attack, but I wasn't sure he looked friendly either. He didn't look as surprised as I felt, and that annoyed me.

"You have the loudest damned energy I've ever seen," he said, folding his arms across his chest.

He was tall and while not broad, he wasn't skinny either; dark-skinned with a shaved head and green eyes. He was, admittedly, very striking. I could see a shoulder holster over his dark t-shirt with a gun, 9mm I guessed, and a knife sheath sticking out of his boot. Armed for bear, ready for battle. Who the hell was this guy?

I kept my muscles tensed as I shifted back into a form that could talk, crouched down and eyeing him.

"Interesting," was all he said.

"Who are you?"

"Who are you?"

I grimaced. "Are you five?" I snapped. "I asked you a damn question."

Instead of answering, he stared at me.

I stared back.

We didn't say anything.

This was going to take all fucking day.

"You're on my hunt." This was what he said instead of answering my question, but hell, we had to start somewhere.

"You work for Pre-Tech?" I asked, narrowing my eyes, which considering how narrow they had already been...

He nodded slowly. "They hired me."

Well, then, that made sense. It took them a week to hire me because they'd hired someone else, someone who sucked.

"Their mistake," I said with a somewhat nasty smile. I didn't like surprises.

His dark brows drew down. "So who the hell are you?"

So far, he hadn't shown any sign that he was going to attack me so I slowly got to my feet, though I never took my eyes off him. "You still haven't answered my question." That came out way more petulantly than I wanted it to.

"Now who's five?" he retorted.

My eye twitched. "I know you're not from around here," I finally said. "Everyone around here knows who I am."

He snorted. "Ego much?"

"What?" I said with a shrug. "It's true. You get in the papers often enough… Which clearly you haven't, so who the fuck are you? And *what* the fuck are you, by the way? You smell weirder than anything I've ever encountered."

"I," he began, but I could already tell by the smarmy look on his face that I wasn't going to like his response, "am the guy who was hired to do this job, so fuck off."

I was right. I didn't like that answer.

"Look, asshole," I began, not afraid to be smarmy myself, "if you could have done the job, they wouldn't have hired me."

I could tell that I'd scored on that one.

"Dylan Parker," he finally said. "I'm from California…"

He was still talking, but I tuned him out as soon as my senses caught something. It was hard to tell in human form, but a faint whiff and a small branch-breaking sound had my head whipping around. I held up my hand to make him shut up, but he apparently thought it was sign language for 'just keep yapping' and so he did.

I tried to zone in on what I was picking up on, gesturing again and being ignored again.

"Shut up!" I finally hissed, and he frowned. Then his eyes darted from side to side, and I knew that he'd just picked up on something too.

Whirling to my left, I saw something colored wrong dart away. "Fuck," I growled, throwing my body forward. Cat paws hit the ground and took off running, but I already knew that I was too late.

It was the jaguar, I could smell her, but the thing had a

head start and a better idea of her escape route. After several minutes, hearing the big dude crashing through the branches behind me, I skidded to a stop. I was human again and in his face in moments. He was only about 6' so we were eye-to-eye.

"Idiot!" I all but shouted. "Where did you learn how to hunt? An online course? The Idiot's Guide to Hunting?"

"That thing is just too damn crafty," he shouted back. "If it was like any normal animal, I would have caught it already!"

"Not as stupid as you are," I growled. "I knew something was out there, and you wouldn't shut your trap long enough for me to narrow in on it until it was too late and it was gone! I should hogtie you and leave you at a convenient tree stump, praying a search-and-rescue group with more skill than you will eventually find you!" Whirling around, I started to storm off.

Parker made the mistake of grabbing my arm. "Hey, lady," he began but didn't get to finish whatever chauvinistic response was about to come out of his mouth because using the momentum he started, I spun back to him and then drove the heel of my hand down on the bridge of his nose. I knew I had broken it, but he was lucky I didn't uppercut and drive that bone up into his brain.

No surprise, he let go. Stumbling back, he held his bleeding nose and cursed profusely as I was able to make my storming-off exit like I'd originally intended.

Once I was back in my car, I brought out my phone and dialed Pre-Tech. I got Wilson.

"This is Dakota. I want to talk to Ms. Hill," I said none-too-kindly.

"I'm sorry, but Ms. Hill is not available right now."

"I don't give a fuck. Interrupt whatever the hell she's in the middle of and put her on the phone. There's a problem."

There was a pause. "What is the nature of the problem?"

A growl boiled up from my throat before I could stop it. "I'd rather discuss that with the woman who signed my check."

Another long pause that did nothing to quell my temper. "I'm sorry, but I cannot allow you to talk to Ms. Hill at this time. If the problem persists, please call me again and make me aware of what the issue is."

She hung up. The bitch hung up on me.

I really didn't want to rip the wheel off the steering column, so I sat in the quiet for a few moments before I started the engine. I headed for home but dialed Pre-Tech several times on the way. They didn't answer this time, which just pissed me off more. They must have had some idea what my 'problem' was and were now going to dodge me. That was sure as hell no way to do business, and my not-that-great opinion of them got even more not-so-great.

By the time I reached the house, I hadn't had any better luck getting through to Pre-Tech.

I walked through the door, and Edward seemed to materialize before me. "Where'd you go?" he asked, sounding grumpy. He'd probably been getting an earful all morning.

"Working," I replied tersely, shouldering my way past him and heading for my room.

It must've been feeding time or something, because I could hear all of the dogs outside barking their heads off. On edge as I was, the sound just drove through me like an ice pick at the base of my skull.

"Well, we could have used your help here," he said, following me for some reason.

"You're not going to fucking start too, are you?" I snapped, spinning to face him. I caught him so off guard that he actually stumbled back a step. "I don't want to hear another damned word out of your damned mouth if you want to keep all of your body parts together," I growled, and apparently my look was enough to get through to him. He said nothing, although he didn't walk away either. I felt his eyes driving into my back as I walked down the hall and turned into my room.

Buster hopped off the bed as soon as he saw me, leaning his head against my leg.

I sat on the floor right there and let him lean against me. I couldn't believe how fast he had gotten attached to me, nor could I believe how fast I had gotten attached to him. That blockhead rested against my shoulder as I took a breath, appreciating the calming feeling that this sudden new presence in my life brought.

The calm didn't last too long as the barking from outside drove into me again. "I need to get out of here," I said, despite the fact that I'd just come home. "Come on." I stood up and grabbed his leash. We went out to the car and drove away.

It was pretty spur of the moment, so I stopped at the store and got a can of dog food and some paper bowls. Then we went to the office. Madison wasn't in the front when we walked in, so Buster and I snuck past her to the corridor that ran off behind her desk. My office was back there, barely used, and we slipped into it. I put the paper dishes down, filled one with water from a bottle I'd bought with the other stuff and the other with dog food. Buster ate noisily while I sunk down onto the blank space beside the door. I probably should have gotten a couch or something, but the floor was fine for now.

I enjoyed the quiet. Buster's eating didn't bother me. Something about making the dog happy made me happy. I didn't get it, but there it was.

Time passed. I wasn't sure how long it was, but my door opened a crack and when I saw Sadie's face, I knew it had to be after dark. I angled my head to look at her upside-down, and she tilted her head at me.

"Are you alright?" she asked with genuine concern, then peeked around the edge to see Buster looking at her uncertainly. "Why is there a dog here?"

"He's mine," I replied simply, still looking at her upside down. "We're hiding."

She looked at me again with a faint smirk. "Edward again?"

I make a disgruntled noise and flattened back out. "And Lorelei and the house and all the dogs..." Sighing, I put my forearm across my eyes. "I just couldn't take it anymore."

"You never come into this office to work, have you noticed that?" she asked, but I didn't hear any animosity in her voice. I knew she didn't mind. My job wasn't really the type that required being in an office, after all.

"Can I sleep here tonight?" I asked, pulling my arm away to look at her again.

She smiled. "Is the dog staying too?"

"Is that a problem?"

"No," she finally said, "just make sure he doesn't make a mess or scare any of our clients."

I ignored the irony of one dog scaring people at a vampire-owned business.

She left me alone then and went back to her own office, because as boss, hers was a job that did a lot of work in the office. I didn't know how she could stand it. Quite frankly, if I had to look at these same four walls that much then I would go entirely insane. Then again, I was starting to feel that way about the four walls of my own bedroom.

Buster laid down next to me, noisily licking the remaining food off his jowls as he settled on the floor.

Maybe my office wasn't so bad, after all.

CHAPTER SEVEN

Buster woke me the next morning. I peeled my eyelids open to look at his face and could almost see the panic in his gaze as he hopped around. It only took me a few moments to realize what the issue was. I grabbed his leash, and he bounded for the door as I groaned and creaked in the process of standing.

I took him for a walk, and it didn't take long for business to get settled. Checking the time, I knew that I was due to help out at the ceremony site so we hopped into the car.

The ceremony and reception were taking place in the city's park, which was a large, protected tract of forest that, unlike much of the rest of the forest, was legally not allowed to be sold so all the preternatural species could use it for all kinds of things. The wolves had their full moon runs, the witches had their rituals, and the vampires did their... vampire things.

It was also used for all sorts of other more boring things, like weddings.

Large squares of laminated wood were being laid down over the grass to make a dance floor as Buster and I walked up. Madison and Chance were helping, since they weren't vampires and were thus awake. I also saw Jackson and Nykk and Daniel. There were a few I didn't recognize, but one of them saw Buster and looked concerned.

"That's a Pitbull, isn't it?" he asked hesitantly.

"A mix," I agreed.

He eyed me and then the dog again. "Are you sure he's safe to be around so many people?"

I eyed him back. "If you have any idea who I am, do you really think he's the risky one?"

The man blinked and seemed to guess who I was by my statement, so he just turned and got back to work. I did tie Buster's leash to a tree, giving him a drink of water before I went to help. I made sure he was somewhere that I could keep an eye on him from everywhere I might work, not because I was worried what he might do to others but to make sure people were nice to him.

We laid out the dance floor and then set up several circular tables with accompanying chairs. I left the table settings and bows on chairs to Madison, because she was a girl. I was... Well, I was anatomically female but didn't have certain 'girl genes' that she clearly had, so I left her to do her business whilst I handled the grunt work.

By the time we were done, I had to admit that it looked nice. The sun was starting to dim, and I knew it would soon be time.

After collecting Buster, we left the site and headed back to the house. I wasn't enthused by the idea but knew I had no choice. Neither Edward nor Lorelei were in sight as I entered, so the dog and I went straight to my bedroom. I made sure he had water and then went to take a shower. (At least I had my own bathroom, although it wasn't attached to my room.)

After my shower, I got dressed for the wedding. I was the best man, so I made sure to look a little less awful than at other times. I wore black slacks and blazer with a white button-down, the top button undone with a white gold chain around my neck. I owned very little jewelry, but the occasion seemed to call for it.

The dog was snoring on my bed by the time I had my shoes on and was ready to go. I put his food out, and that woke him up quick enough.

On my way out of my room, I ran (almost literally) into Edward.

"You didn't come home last night," he said, apparently by way of greeting.

"Nope," I replied flatly. I saw the sun setting through the window. "Are you guys ready to go?"

He looked at me sidelong for a few moments. "We will be in a few minutes."

I nodded and went to the kitchen. Opening the fridge, I considered starting to drink now but decided that if I was caught, it would make the home situation so much more unbearable. I might have to take up residence in my office permanently. So I drank a glass of water and waited, leaning back against the kitchen counter until the pair of them walked in.

The air was tense, and we all spoke as little as possible during the somewhat awkward car ride back to the park.

By now, it was fully dark, so all of the guests, vampires included, were arriving. There wasn't really assigned seating, so I let the pair of them go find a seat while I went off in search of people that didn't hate me at the moment.

☾O☽

The moon was just shy of full—so no surprise shifting at the party—and illuminated the summer sky. It was a little humid for my tastes, but tolerable. I found Vance waiting nervously by the podium set at the 'head' of the dance floor.

"You look nervous," I remarked, because I am, in fact, the Queen of Tact.

"I'm still having trouble with crowds and attention," he commented, and I knew what he meant. Since that...trouble he had a few months ago, and becoming a vampire, parts of his personality had shifted a bit. He was still in the process of adapting to them. Adapting to major life changes was something I could understand.

The pastor of the local congregational church walked up and smiled at me. I nodded back. I went to the Episcopal, so I didn't really know him.

Then we stood and waited. Vance paced around a little.

My phone beeped, and I looked at it. It was a text from Sadie: "I'm almost there. Tell Vance not to pace."

I snorted a laugh. "OK"

"Vance!" I called. "Get your ass in place, your wife is coming."

He looked at me dryly. "You're such a classy woman."

I smirked. "She says stop pacing."

"How did she…" he began but then trailed off, shaking his head. "Never mind." He found his place to the left of the pastor, and I took my place beside him.

Everyone else had apparently heard us and all took their seats. It worked out rather well, really. Inside of a couple of minutes, I heard a pair of car doors shut. D and Cassandra (his creepy sweet vampire girlfriend) came up and took their seats, followed by Chance, who smirked in my direction, undoubtedly thinking of the bachelor party. We both may still have been a little hungover. Another couple of minutes and I watched Madison enter the clearing in a red dress. She crossed the dance floor/aisle and stood opposite me and Vance, and then the DJ started some music—not the bridal march—and Sadie crossed the floor, joining Vance.

He stared at her in a way that I don't think I've ever seen a man stare at a woman. And her, well, for a woman looking on the short road to a century, she looked really damn good in a strapless cream-colored gown with…sparkly things on it that I was sure had a name but fuck if I knew what it was. She had pretty red ribbon-like things in her hair, a red that matched Vance's shirt and Madison's dress.

The music stopped, and the preacher started.

I knew I liked Sadie and Vance for a reason: the ceremony was short and not drowning in sap. Their personally written vows were even funny. Vance added in some of our one-liners from the bachelor party.

I was proud.

They were declared husband and wife, and the whole clearing lit up with applause, wolf howls, literal cat calls, and any number of other frightening sounds that a group of preternatural beings can make. It was actually kind of fun. But again, I wasn't going to admit it to anyone. I wasn't supposed to be enjoying a wedding, after all. I had a reputation to maintain.

Once the noise died down and Vance stopped checking if Sadie's tonsils were pointed too, the DJ kicked up some music. Vance led her straight to the center of the floor. Madison and I appropriately moved to the edges to watch the newlywed-but-not-really-newlyweds start dancing.

"Do you ever think about getting married?" Edward asked me as I sat down at the table with him and Lorelei. Apparently, he was going to try to make small talk so we could get past this Thing we had going on. I wasn't sure that was his best tactic…

I looked at him like I was nuts. "Hi, have you met me?"

The pair of them laughed quietly, and it didn't sound forced, so there was that. She gave him a look that made me wonder if they'd talked about it, but I didn't want to know. I wasn't totally done being annoyed at them yet.

Turning away from the pair, I looked at Sadie and Vance on the floor. They had the good grace to not be mauling each other, but it was hard to disguise the disgusting amount of adoration in their eyes. It was one of those sights that made you want to turn away and yet you couldn't manage to do so at the same time. I was…a little jealous, if I was to tell the truth. Most people thought I was little better than the monsters I hunted, but I could be as human as anyone else. I got lonely. I hadn't found many people who could tolerate me, and those that did never seemed to last…so I guess they couldn't really tolerate me after all.

Maybe some people are just meant to be alone. Over all, I preferred it that way anyways. I don't like anyone, remember?

The song ended, and the DJ invited everyone else onto the floor. Madison dragged Chance, whose grin was the sort that said he really didn't mind. Jackson dragged Nykk, and she earnestly looked like she was being dragged, but the circle of his arms made that look vanish. D and Cassandra. Edward and Lorelei. Daniel and Elena. And then a few others I recognized and the dates they had brought, whose names I didn't know.

Eventually, it seemed like I was the only one still on my ass.

I took a deep breath and got up, moving a little further from the light and into the darkness of the tall trees surrounding the event. I didn't like the conflicting feelings brewing in the center of my body. I could still hear the music loud and clear, since I didn't move that far away, but enough to take in some darkness and a little less of the 'white noise' that comes with so many people.

That lasted…not very long.

From the other side of the clearing, there came a scream. My head shot around. It came again a heartbeat later, and I sprinted back to the reception. A flurry of activity was taking place on the other side of the dance floor but before I could get over there, another shout of anger came from a different side. People leapt out of the way of…something. The people toward the center of the dance floor whirled, and again when a scream came from another corner.

Out of a group of maybe fifty people, the cluster of

sound had moved three times in maybe three minutes.

I followed my instinct for when I feel threatened, and my body shifted to the form of the mountain lion. I shrieked. Cougars don't roar like most other cats, they scream. I let my voice be known to whatever this threat was and as soon as my nose was a cat's, all of my senses exploded. I took in the scents of all the different people, but there was something else. Something...foreign to this group. Something strange... and yet familiar, although in the heat of the moment, I couldn't make the connection.

My scream apparently got the threat's attention because it bounded to the center of the dance floor where I could see it and it could see me. I could barely recognize what I was looking at while it raced for me. *The Island of Doctor Moreau* jumped in my head for an instant before I leaped to meet it, and my brain stopped racing to fantasy.

Jaguar.

Chapter Eight

Claws sunk into my body, and mine sank into hers. We crashed hard to the dance floor as people jumped out of our way, shrieking and roaring. Fur leaped in fits and the scent of jaguar filled my nose, but the body I was grappling with didn't feel completely like a cat's. My brain couldn't process it, because I knew it was a cat and I was hunting a cat and here it fucking was. I didn't have much time to figure it out as I felt jaws snapping for my neck. I yanked my head away before trying to get to her neck instead.

I don't love many people. I do love Sadie and Vance. I won't say it to them, but they're my family, and I had every intention of chewing this thing to bits for ruining their night.

Blurs of motion suddenly flew over me, and I knew that vampires were at work, the scent of my brother mixed in with it. Males hands—six, if I could see correctly—grabbed the beast, yanking her off of me with their supernatural strength. I almost had the chance to get a hold of her neck, but as she flung herself back at them, she was suddenly out of their grip.

How the fuck did that happen?

My head was at an awkward angle as I stared back at the scene, trying to flip back onto my feet. The boys were all about to go for the beast, but something happened. She just stared at them, and I saw them all...freeze. It was the only word I could use to describe it. Their eyes were full of anger and fire, but their bodies weren't moving. I too was frozen for a moment trying to figure out what was going on.

D's arm was the first to break the invisible ice, cracking through whatever was holding them captive with a vicious roar. Blurs came in from the edges of my vision, and I think there were female vampires in the midst of them, leaping onto the thing's back. I thought I recognized the tough-as-nails lead warden of the vampire coven. Not a woman to mess with, and that's coming from me, but an arm swung and sent both forms flying away into the tables.

I saw their descent slow and sensed a telekinetic at work while people were popping in and out of view, rescued by a teleporter to safer areas. There were several humans among the group, after all, and they wouldn't be able to do anything when shifters and vampires were getting tossed around like ragdolls.

It was then that I saw the beast a little clearer for a moment, looking like an animal but standing on two legs as she threw her attackers off.

Is this my hunt?

Of course it was.

I got back on my feet and was about to leap onto her, but the thing whirled toward the tables where I saw the tall, lanky Chance standing and growling in front of Madison. The beast, looking like a cat, seemed to be as pissed off about the smell of a tiger as she was about the sound of a cougar. She jumped at him, but then... Was that a jump? She moved so fast that I began to suspect there wasn't any actual jumping taking place...

Chance grabbed the thing, and they fell back into the table, but claws against Chance's human form—normal shifters took too long to find their animal forms—didn't make for a good pairing. I heard Madison cry out. I crossed the distance in a handful of bounds and was onto the jaguar's back, which was the only thing I could think of her as, digging claws into her and throwing my weight to the side. I managed to pull her off balance enough to get her away from Chance and Madison, while peripherally aware of Elena (teleporter) bringing Cassandra (healer vampire) to their sides to check them over before blinking them away.

The jaguar's flesh remained under my claws as she reached behind herself in a way that no cat possibly could and ripped me off, throwing me into a table. I screamed as the table broke and we both collided with the ground. I was surging back to my feet when I heard singing.

Posey Kai—Jackson's FBI agent partner who looked like an anime character—was standing fearlessly in the middle of the dance floor with her eyes focused on the beast. A beautiful, wordless melody poured from her lips, and the beast turned slowly toward her, like she was spellbound. And I was sure that she was as I felt it in my own bones. Moving sluggishly, I tried to get up and advance toward the jaguar again.

Vance wasn't caught by Posey's spell and leaped onto the monster. She roared and shook him, the magic broken. He was tossed into Posey, and they both fell back to the floor. I was almost on the jaguar again, but she popped out of sight, and I was sure she was teleporting. She almost landed on top of Chris, one of Vance's other friends, who jumped away and used her cryokinesis to ice the spot under the jaguar's feet. Her claws didn't help her as she started flailing and slid back to where Jackson was standing in front of a table protecting the humans. His hands were out and glowing red with his inner fire, making the jaguar scream in pain as bits of fur lit up.

Fire was apparently her limit—it was for many a creature—because she took off, clearly making a break for it. Without having to say a word to each other, Edward and I were right behind her. He had joined me in big cat form, and we were racing through trees, lacing around the woods and trying to keep the scent. We couldn't keep her in sight once we hit the forest, but we could always count on the smell…

…or could we?

I skidded to a halt when I realized that I'd lost her. Edward stopped a few steps ahead, almost going headfirst into a tree.

More slowly, I proceeded forward in my original path, but I didn't pick up the scent again. I backtracked myself to where our claw marks marked the spot. I tried another direction but didn't get it. My frustration began to cloud my senses until Edward shifted to human.

"We have to go back," he said.

I shrieked, but I agreed with him. I wasn't sure how long it had been (as cats and watches don't mix) and slunk back to the reception, still as a kitty because why bother sulking in human form when cats are made to slink?

The disaster was still in the process of being organized when we got back. The cops in the black-and-whites were already there, and so was…

I shifted to human just so I could spit curses.

"What the fuck are you doing here?!" I shouted, storming up to that…guy who was jacking my hunt.

"You are such a pleasant person," Parker drawled. "That thing was here. I'm after that thing. So I'm here. It's really not that hard of an equation. I don't even think it would qualify for basic algebra."

My hand clenched into a fist and I started forward, my shoulder cocking back, but Sam—who happened to be standing right there—cleared her throat, and I thought better of it. Well, I changed my mind, at least. Too many witnesses that were also cops. I ground my teeth together trying to keep the kitty fangs from coming back when I heard Lorelei shouting at Edward for taking risks that weren't his to take. Oh, geez, that was gonna be another mess when we got home.

Tuning them out, I returned my focus to that guy and Sam. Sneering at him, I grabbed my ex's elbow and dragged her away. "Stay, creep boy," I spat. "Girl talk." A moment later, I muttered to her, "Is it just me or is this really bad?"

"I'd call this really bad," she agreed. "That was the thing you're hunting, I'm betting?"

I snorted. "You think? I can't imagine there's a whole lot of murderous jaguars running around right now. Did you get anything on the victim? Was it a cat attack?"

Sam nodded reluctantly. "Looks like, yes. Victim's name was Ally Walker. Small-time drug dealer in the area. A fact that doesn't help narrow down the list of potential suspects, given that drug dealers are usually the cheeriest bunch of folk."

I rubbed the back of my neck. I wasn't just hunting a cat, that was pretty obvious now, but that didn't mean I knew what I *was* after. I knew she was doing things that a regular cat couldn't do, but she looked like a jaguar. She smelled like a jaguar...mostly.

"So..." I hesitated, because I hated that I was about to ask what I was about to ask. You know how they say it's better to beg forgiveness than ask permission? Yeah, I usually try to live by that, so the next words tasted bad. "Can I still keep hunting this thing?" The cops were too close, and I felt obnoxiously compelled to check.

"Yes," she answered with far less hesitation than I expected. "I already talked to the captain."

I blinked, genuinely surprised. I had expected to have to fight for this one. "Well. Uh. That's...great. Thanks. I'll, uh, keep you informed."

She smirked, knowing me too well. "You're welcome." With that, she walked off.

I was still staring after her when Parker appeared beside me. I smelled him coming, but with so many people milling around, I didn't actually think much about it until he spoke. "I might as well draw freaking hearts over your head."

"What the hell is your problem?" I snapped, whirling around to face him.

"So, cops still letting you hunt this thing?" He smiled smugly.

"*Me*, yes," I replied pointedly. "You are going to back… wherever it is you came from and you're going to leave me alone, because this is my business and not yours now. I'm the one that the cops know and gave permission to, and you're just the guy that I can get arrested for interfering."

He lost his smug look. "I was still hired to do this too."

It was my turn to look smug. "Now it's a police matter."

"You're not police."

"Closer than you are," I replied easily. "You go away. This is not a place for you because it's friends and family. And the hunt is where I'm going."

He folded muscular arms across his chest. "You can't stop me."

I grinned. I've been told it's a pretty frightening expression. "Watch me." Turning my face to the sky, I sprouted my wings and flapped until I caught a current and soared away. No one would wonder where I went; they never did. This was me we were talking about, and they knew what I was like. Edward and Lorelei would find their way home, and I had little desire to be around for the new grudge match.

Of course, home was where I went, but I'd get there first and could barricade myself in my room.

Buster barked when the bedroom door opened but stopped as soon as he saw me. He hopped off the bed and trotted forward to where I knelt before him, scratching his ears. "Finally, someone I'm actually happy to see," I said, and he snorted like he understood. I took him outside and let him handle his business before we went back into my room and

I locked the door.

I sat on my bed and pulled my laptop on my lap, opening up a map of Adelheid. I looked it over and mentally plotted the points for Pre-Tech, where I found the corpse, and then the reception. The last was pretty far away from the other two, which didn't make much sense for a jaguar. They're territorial. Jaguars are also ambush hunters, which would make no sense for attacking a wedding reception full of people.

"What is going on, Buster?" I asked. Yes, I asked the dog. They usually know more than people. Animals in general, at least. People suck.

Alright, so what did she seem to do? She looked like a cat, mostly, but she seemed to jump around way faster than any creature should. She also seemed to have some kind of mind control. How did that even happen? I was pretty sure she was teleporting, but it was so damned odd, so maybe it was something else. Telekinesis? Super-speed? But with some kind of mind control? Nothing made sense, and I couldn't reconcile what I had seen at the reception with what my brain knew.

The area around Pre-Tech seemed a more likely fit to be her territory. The reception was an outlier I couldn't yet explain, but if I was going to find something, it would be around there. I hoped.

Buster and I curled up and went to sleep. About an hour later, we woke up when Edward and Lorelei got home. They were still shouting at each other. "This is why we should stay single, man," I murmured to the dog snoring by my feet.

☾◯☽

The next day, I woke up late and made sure it was silent in the house before I took Buster out. (Since I had to force him to get up, I was sure he didn't mind.) When he was done and we got back inside, I got him settled down and readied myself to go back out. When I heard someone—whichever one of my lovely housemates it was, I didn't know—moving around the house, I decided to go out the window.

My first stop was Pre-Tech. That was the epicenter of the issue, so that was where I would start. Yes, I'd done it before, but sometimes a fresh look reaped new rewards, especially with new information. I started 'patrolling' the area in kitty form, trying to use some sort of outward spiraling search pattern to see if I could pick up any traces of anything. As it amounted to nothing, I went home and tried again the next day.

It was on day two that I got lucky, so to speak.

On a farther-out loop of my semi-haphazard spiral, I stopped short when I picked up the sudden and stupidly strong scent of a jaguar. My muscles tensed ahead of my conscious adrenaline reaction, and some sixth sense had me leaping back just before that damn cat came flying at me. She hit the dirt where I had just been, and I shrieked in annoyance.

The return noise echoed my sentiments as she took a swipe at me with claws out, the move reminding me more of a human fighter's haymaker than a wild cat. I dodged back before leaping forward, straight-up tackling the other cat. The fact that I actually caught her this time surprised me almost enough to let her go.

I kept my weight pressing down, lunging for her throat. She tried to shake me off before making her own attempt for my neck. As we tussled, she tried to thrust her weight and throw me off. I felt her back claws under my belly and knew she was trying to disembowel me, but I would let her have about as much success as a kitten with a ball of yarn who does the same thing. I leaped back far enough to get her claws away from me.

She surged to her feet and lunged for me. I swung my paw and knocked her in the face. She hissed and did that popping-porting thing. She landed on my back. I shrieked and reared, knocking her into a convenient tree trunk. She fell off me. I whirled around and jumped for her, landing on her scrambling form and going for her throat. Before I reached it, I felt the trembling of muscle under me. For a few moments, I saw the cat form…shift. Not completely, but I saw the cat body shift just enough to look bipedal.

Almost human.

Then came that hocus-pocus she'd used at the reception. There was a soft, short breezy sound and she was gone. I hit the ground, but had been dazed before even that happened, trying to process everything. There was a lot of it, too. I was too shocked to even pursue. This was all even more confusing than I thought, and it had been pretty fucking confusing.

There was some human in there, but that was no shifter.

No *normal* shifter, at least.

CHAPTER NINE

I didn't even bother trying to call Pre-Tech this time, I just went right back to their building and pressed the buzzer, which was where I promptly got shot down. When the tin-voice asked who was there, I told them.

The speaker went silent and so was the door, which was supposed to buzz and let me in.

"Fuckers," I muttered. But if they were refusing my calls, I could hardly be surprised. Stepping away from the door, I walked around the building. It wasn't like I hadn't seen plenty of it lately, but this time, it was with an eye for entries. And, in a word, there weren't many. There was the front door and then a single back exit, but that didn't look any easier to get through. With an eye for where the security cameras were, I found what I thought to be a blind spot and shifted form.

Now I was a much shorter woman with curly blonde hair and dimples.

In my far more girlish and less threatening appearance, I approached the door again. I pressed the buzzer, but I didn't even get a 'hello' this time. Frowning, I wondered if the timing was too telling (there was a camera above the panel, so I assumed they'd look) or if the blind spot hadn't been so blind.

I snorted in annoyance and shifted right there in front of their camera, muttering. Walking away, I eyed the building again. There were no windows on the bottom floor. The place was set up like steel-and-beige-cement fortress. I probably should've reflected on that more when I'd shown up the first time. Apparently, I was getting lax in my old age.

Stepping further back, I saw windows around the second floor and then spotted what looked like another door on the roof. That was probably considered the less threatening point of entry, and thus that was my next target. With no apparent handholds—cement, remember?—I took to wings and flew up to the roof. Landing on human feet, I approached the door and took the handle.

It was unlocked and swung open. I snorted. With no other buildings around it, who would expect someone to come to the roof from the outside? For a preternaturally-oriented business, they weren't too bright.

Once inside, I let the door shut quietly and found myself in a dark stairwell. As a safety precaution, I shifted to a new form. This one was of average height, average weight, with plain brown hair and unremarkable brown eyes. Basically, I was designed to blend in. I let myself wear a white lab coat.

I'm sure you're wondering about the clothing shifting. I do own clothing and wear them, because holding specific clothing form can be exhausting. My 'regular' form takes little effort and even less if I don't have to 'do' the clothes. My magic somehow changes what is touching my body with me, but it takes extra effort. I am a really good multi-tasker, basically, but if I had to keep the new form and clothes too long, I would grow very exhausted. Lesson over.

With decent vision in the dark, I walked down the stairs and let myself into the second floor, but it looked entirely like...offices. Boring old corporate-style offices. That didn't interest me at all so I stepped back into the stairwell, better lit now, and went to the bottom floor. Peeking out through the door, I saw that the corridor was empty and walked out. It wasn't far at all along the corridor before I looked to either side and saw glass walls giving a great view into the labs.

What was I looking for? I had no idea. I just knew that shit was going on that was very not okay, and that it started here.

I walked along, looking to either side and examining the labs within. There weren't many employees, but those that I saw looked very...industrious in their lab coats and clear glasses, tapping away at computers or using droppers to put things in vials. It was practically a commercial for a pharmaceutical company...or a sci-fi movie.

Engrossed as I was by the rather bizarre scenes, I caught the approaching scent behind me too late.

"Excuse me?"

The voice behind me belonged to a man. Turning around, I saw a security guard. The security in this place was impressive. He was average height, slightly overweight. His brows knit as he looked at my chest. I might have been offended, but I realized quickly that he was seeking a name badge.

I played along and looked down, smacking my collar bone and gasping. "Shit, I must have left it in the bathroom," I said, turning and walking away as if I had a great purpose that I had to see to. He started to say something, but I was already around the corner. Since it had been this direction or through him, the choices in which way to go had been slim.

Once around the corner, I leaned briefly against the wall and snickered.

"Do you work here?"

"Oh, what the—" I began, whirling on this new voice that had snuck up on me. I stopped short when I saw that he was wearing a lab coat. That was when the idea came to me about what I needed, which was one of these little lab rat people. I smiled slowly, and fear bloomed in his eyes. "Say nothing."

"What are you—"

I grabbed him by the throat, and my preternatural strength was clear. I didn't do enough to do damage, but I made my point. "Didn't I just say to say nothing?" I said. "You people are messing with shit you shouldn't be here, and you're going to do your civic duty and help me figure out what that is."

His dark brows knit.

"You gonna do what I say?" His head jerked as much as my hand would allow in something that resembled a nod. Releasing his neck, I stepped back. I looked down the hallway and contemplated which direction to go. The door I had seen from the backside of the building appeared to be down this hall, so I gripped his upper arm and began dragging him to it.

The sign over it read "emergency exit, alarm will sound," so I looked around it until I found the small box with wires at the bottom. I kneeled, dragging my captive with me, and tore the wires out. No alarms sounded. Ha, for all the money to make their little fortress, that was one failsafe they missed.

I dragged him through the door. It wasn't until we were free of the building that he seemed to find enough bravery, or fear, to get his voice back.

"What are you doing with me?" he asked hesitantly.

"I'm not going to kill you." I was sure that would be reassuring. "You are going to help me."

There was a long pause. "Who are you?"

As we walked, I shifted back into my normal form and was glad to let that bit of concentration go. He didn't say anything and probably didn't recognize me, since why would the lab rats know anything about hiring hunters?

Coming around to the parking lot, I was hauling him to my car when who would show up but...

"Fucker!"

"Glad to see you too, Dakota," Parker said with a smug grin as he leaned back against my car, arms folded over his chest. The odd scent that always accompanied him drifted past my nose, and I again tried to figure out what it was but couldn't.

"Don't call me that." His brows rose, silently asking what he should call me. "Don't call me anything. I don't want to see you anymore."

He ignored that. "Who's your friend?"

"Hell if I know," I replied. I began mentally calculating how to move him away from my car and drag my captive into it.

"You can't be telling me that you actually kidnapped someone," he laughed. His words said he was appalled, but the grin and the laugh said he was anything but. His white teeth flashed, and I debated knocking all of them out. "I thought you were too well-behaved for something like that."

I snorted. "Get the hell away from my car."

His dark brow rose. "Make me."

"What is this, elementary school?"

"We both know neither of us went there."

That actually drew me up short for a moment. I blinked. How did he know that I hadn't gone to elementary school? (They didn't have it four hundred years ago.) And what was he that he hadn't either? I didn't smell vampire on him, and he only looked maybe thirty. Could he be fae? Didn't smell like a fae, but they were slippery fish.

My grip went lax on the Pre-Tech guy, and he had actually started to slip away before I realized how distracted the other hunter had made me. Snarling, my hand snaked out without fully looking and grabbed him by the back of his neck. I marched him around to the back of my car and put him inside where I put the creatures I hunted. There was a grate that would keep him from accessing the car locks. I shut the hatch door.

With Pre-Tech guy taken care of, I went back to my

driver's-side door and my other problem. "Move, asshole."

His dark gaze held mine. "Think he has information about where the creature is?" he asked instead of following my order.

"I think he has information about what the creature is," I replied flatly. "Now, move."

He didn't.

I hit him. First in the gut until he bent forward and then up into his face. Coughing and cursing, he fell to one knee with his hand against the dirt. Why had he not seen that coming, after our last encounter? I opened my car door, knocking him in the side of the head, then stepped over him to get in. I shut the door; he was fortunate to be far enough away to avoid getting hit again. Far enough away for me to start the car and drive off without denting my fender.

❨○❩

It wasn't until I got to the police station that I realized he had followed me. Somehow, he had gotten to his own car and snagged right on my tail. Admittedly, that impressed me. It also impressed me that I hadn't even noticed I was being tailed.

"Here, really?" he asked disdainfully. "So it's true, you really are too damned cozy with the police. How can you be a good hunter when you have to play by the rules like them?"

"How can you not end up in prison if you play against them?" I snapped back, dragging the very befuddled and rather frightened scientist in with me.

The infuriating man followed me. "You're going to get arrested for kidnapping."

To that, I didn't reply.

The uniformed officer at the desk recognized me and

although she gave a curious look to my 'guests,' she waved me past. I paused to point to the other guy. "Arrest him, would you?" She looked even more confused and didn't arrest him, but to his sputtering outrage, she told him he couldn't go in. I just laughed as I left him behind.

"What is going on?" Sam asked as she came out to see me. Although it was getting late in the day, it was still too early for the vampires.

"This guy works at Pre-Tech," I explained, dragging him around and dropping him in a seat.

She eyed me and then him and then me. "Okay..." she said slowly.

I took a quick look at him, but the guy didn't look like he was gonna try to bolt again. In fact, his passivity was kind of surprising. Maybe I was more frightening than I thought. Now that he was in view of the police, I also thought he looked...guilty, perhaps?

"I was running around Pre-Tech labs and looking for that jaguar. Guess what? I found her, and do you know what? She's not just a jaguar. She partial-shifted, but not in any way I've seen a real shifter do. She also is a teleporter, I'm sure of it now. There may be more, but that's what I've seen for myself. I don't know what Pre-Tech was doing, but they were fucking with things that should not be fucked with."

"You've always had such a way with words," Sam drawled.

I smirked. "So I borrowed my...friend here from his work day and brought him straight here so he could help us understand."

She eyed me. I eyed her back. We both damn well knew what I had done, but if he didn't press charges, she'd never tell.

We turned our eyes to him, and he swallowed audibly. "I don't know what she's talking about," he tried. "This...person just showed up and made me come here."

"I'm aware of her brand of persuasion," Sam said with a small smile. "However, I also know that while she's a great many things, many of them not good—"

"Hey."

"—I know that 'liar' is not one of them."

"Gee, thanks." It was such fun to have to keep working with an ex-lover. Maybe that's why I'd worked so hard to not have many exes.

He was silent as he stared between us. Sam and I did our best to look intimidating, arms folded over our chests as we stood and stared. After a few more moments, I actually watched a human body deflate.

"I'm not being paid enough," he murmured. "Pre-Tech wanted to understand what made shifters work, and they wanted to replicate it. Maybe make a stronger being."

"Human testing?"

"Half-human," he said. He was still mumbling, like he didn't have the energy (or the guts) to move his mouth fully to form the words. "We had a jaguar and we had a human, but we didn't kidnap anyone." At this, he gave me a telling look. "She was a volunteer."

My brain felt like it was going to bleed. I just couldn't piece together all of the words that he was using and form them into something that made the slightest bit of sense. "Why would anyone volunteer for something like that?" And that was putting that question nicely, I thought. You would have to be a total psycho to want to do shit like that.

"Someone who wanted to get out of sight for a while, I think," he said. "I wasn't really involved much in that part of the process, but she scared me."

"More or less than I do?" I asked, deciding this was a fair scale.

He stared at me. "I'm not sure, but I'm pretty sure that

you scare me more."

Sam snorted.

"They were trying to do other things, other psychic powers, but I don't know which ones," he went on. "I wasn't part of that team."

"So what did you do for Pre-Tech?" So far, I'd heard plenty about all the things he hadn't been involved in, but I knew that he worked there so he must have done something for them.

"I'm a phlebotomist," he said. "I was in charge of bloodwork."

Now, it suddenly seemed like he knew more than one would expect. Still, everything he was saying made sense with the things that I had seen.

After a moment, Sam asked, "What's your name?"

"Jack Fletcher."

"Is Pre-Tech full of idiots?" That was from me, and frankly, I thought that it was the more pertinent of the questions. After what he had just told me, it was the only logical conclusion.

He smiled for the first time, although it was feeble. "Possibly?"

I growled quietly. "Must be, because only idiots would think that werewolves aren't scary enough. They might as well have tried to fit some vampire in there too, and maybe some demonic blood while they're at it."

"I wouldn't put it past them..."

"What I don't understand," Sam mused, "is to what end? What does it serve to make a better predator?" She paused, and her face scrunched slightly. It did that when she figured something out, and I recalled in that moment how much I enjoyed seeing that expression and how much I used to tease her about it. "That's kind of a dumb question."

"I'm sure they're liable for some sort of legal action, but that's your area," I told her. "I still have to catch the Frankenstein's Monster that's running loose with a cat-face in Adelheid."

Chapter Ten

We left Fletcher under the watchful eye of the uniformed officers while we went to look through some files.

I had proposed that even though their human test subject volunteered, she was likely gone for longer than anyone anticipated without any word at all. So, we were going to look through the missing person files.

"We can rule out all the men," Sam remarked as she set a stack of file folders down on the table and we took our seats. "And we can rule out anyone under the age of eighteen or over the age of fifty, based on what little description Fletcher gave us."

"And given the description that she scared him and was likely escaping something, we should look at people with criminal records," I pointed out as we started going through the files, pulling free the ones that were obviously not the ones we needed. Just these initial criteria narrowed us down to about four files, because Adelheid didn't have that many missing people. (If she was from out of town, then we were going to hit a whole new problem.)

"Natalia Wilkes," I read off the first name. I looked at her picture. "Fletcher said the woman was white, so not this one." I set that file aside.

"This one was a convicted shoplifter but nothing violent," Sam said, setting hers on top of mine. "I get the feeling that we're looking for violence."

I nodded, because I agreed.

"This one," she said suddenly. "JJ Burke. Drug dealer in the area, specializes in the harder stuff for the preternatural crowd. Violent. She had a warrant out on her." She smirked slightly and handed me the file, which I looked over.

"Territorial," I said and looked over the list of related addresses, such as places she'd been arrested, committed crimes, or had lived. "Can you pull up a map?"

Sam rolled her chair from the table to her computer and called up a map of Adelheid. I looked between the list and the map. On the screen, I drew a line from point to point. Pre-Tech was right at the edge, but there was the body site and even the reception area. "I think we found her," I agreed. "The attacks so far fall into the area that she used to run in and do deals at."

She nodded. "And you know what, the woman you found..." That record was now pulled up. "Also a drug dealer, filed a complaint against Burke for assault. She had tried to move in on Burke's territory and got put in the hospital for it."

"Yeah, I'm definitely feeling this one," I said, making a mental note of the area that was definitely her 'turf.' I was about to go claw it up.

☾○☽

Being the sneaky bastard that I am, I got out of the police station without the other hunter catching on. In fact, I didn't see or hear him on my way out so I assumed he was either being held somewhere annoying or they had managed to oust him. I didn't really care one way or the other, I was just glad that he wasn't going to be bothering me anymore. The last thing I needed was, well, him. I just wanted to do my job and catch the roaming, murderous freak.

I went home. I slipped back in through the window and

checked on Buster. He snored at me, so I moved on and found my brother.

Now with a little time passed and no angry girlfriends in sight, we just had to look at each other to get past the bickering. After all, we always bickered and always got past it. Only the third party was new.

"Bored yet?" I asked with a smirk.

"Whither thou goest, sister," he said, returning my expression.

Keeping an eye out for Lorelei, we managed to sneak out of the house. We drove to the general vicinity of Pre-Tech, although I stayed out of its parking lot. I didn't know what they might have on me and didn't want to deal with any security trouble while I had things to do.

Dressing up in kitty fur, Edward and I began running from point to point, making a circuit of areas that I knew were connected to Burke. We left a few claw marks on trees and in the dirt, making sure we made our presence known. I wanted her to notice, and I wanted to piss her off, because we needed her to show herself. Better armed with knowledge about this thing, Edward and I would be able to catch her. I had my tranquilizer gun on me so when we found her and subdued her enough, I could shift back to get the gun and shoot a couple heavy-dose darts into her ass.

Cats lacked watches, and thus I didn't know how long it had been, but I guessed somewhere around an hour before I heard the telltale sound.

I stopped and Edward realized it a few steps later and stopped as well, backing up to join me as we stood and listened to the forest. After a few more moments, I heard the low, foreign growl again in the sunset-colored forest. My brother and I exchanged looks, and he slunk off to a better ambush position.

She came for me first, apparently having a bone to pick

with me after our last fight. I sidestepped her lunge, if barely, and whirled around to leap at her. Landing on her back, she tried to throw me off, but I weighed as much as she did and it was no easy feat. Edward came running in then and joined the pile, adding his weight to mine.

As he did, I backed off to make the shift to human and get the gun. Knowing what we were up against, I tried to move quickly, but the jaguar teleported out from under him. She reappeared just a few moments later, and Edward jumped at her. She popped out and back again a few feet away. Now I delayed changing forms so I could jump at her myself.

She saw me coming and ported just as I was about to grab her. Not having a soft fleshy body to hit, I went flying past where she had been and headfirst into a tree.

Fortunately, as everyone tells me, my head is really hard. It saved my neck in that I didn't get any brain damage. It did leave me kind of woozy for a moment, though.

Which was worse.

While I staggered back, shaking my fuzzy head from side to side, I heard a roar behind me. Followed by the sound of something...cracking. Something squishing, too.

I spun around so fast that I made myself sick again, the world spinning around me as all four feet barely managed to keep me upright. My feline stomach started shifting like it was going to crawl out of my mouth. I saw the jaguar port away and was about to go stumbling after her, nausea and all, when I saw what had made the cracking noise.

Edward.

He was lying in a pile on the ground. The brown and green under his head was saturated with red. That was a lot of blood in a short span of time, and the world swam around me again. He wasn't moving. I couldn't even tell if I saw his chest rising and falling. All the blood rushed to my ears. Whose pulse was that: mine or his?

Finally snapping out of the moment, I ran to him. I was human when I tumbled to my knees next to him. His unconscious body shifted from cat to human, without him being conscious, and I knew that was a bad sign.

"Frederick," I whimpered. I never whimpered. I also never used his childhood name, but in my terror, it just spilled from my lips. I put my hands on him, trying to find a pulse. I found one, but it was weak. It was his head. I could see the blood spilling from under his skull as I fumbled with my cell phone.

9-1-1. Those three stupid numbers didn't even filter. I called Sam on my speed dial. (I never had been able to delete her.)

"Sam… Sam… It's m-my brother…"

"Dakota? What's wrong? You're…"

"Sam!" I all but shrieked in her ear. "It's my brother!"

☾O☽

"As best we can tell, he's alive because he's preternatural," the doctor said.

We were standing in the hospital corridor. My brother was in the intensive care room just behind us, laying in a bed in a coma with wires and monitors sticking out of him. It was a head injury, and a bad one. The doctor used a lot of words, medical terms, but there was so much static between my ears that I couldn't properly follow what was happening. I just heard the big news: he was in a coma, and they couldn't tell yet if he would ever wake up.

I couldn't remember how I'd been able to tell Sam our location, and I couldn't remember them getting there. My shirt had handprints on it. My hands. My brother's blood. Sam had driven me behind the ambulance and stood with me now.

Footsteps pounded down the hallway.

Lorelei crashed into me. "What happened?!" she demanded of me before repeating the question to the doctor. Her dark eyes glistened with wild panic.

The doctor got up to the word "coma" when Lorelei whirled at me.

"This is your fault!" she shrieked in pitches that would make dogs wince. It would have made me wince if I wasn't numb. "If you weren't always dragging him out on your dangerous business then he wouldn't be here right now! Don't you care about him at all?! He's not a hunter! It's not his job!"

I shoved her. My palms collided with her shoulders and sent her staggering back several steps. Dazed, I wasn't even using as much force as I could.

"Don't you dare!" I screamed. A feline roar backed my words like a double voice. I felt hands grabbing my shoulder and heard the doctor telling me to calm down. I jerked myself free. "He is my brother and he's been my brother longer than he's been your lover. My dangerous profession paid to get your ungrateful ass up here. How dare you!"

I didn't want to think about the fact she might be right. I didn't want to think about the guilt I carried for centuries, thinking that the deaths of my family had been my fault. I didn't want to think about these things. I didn't want to think that I was going to lose him too, and it enraged me that she managed to make me think them.

I spun around toward the doctor, and he stepped back in surprise. "She's not family. Don't let her back in here," I hissed, pushing past him and into my brother's room while Lorelei shrieked and sputtered incoherently behind me.

CHAPTER ELEVEN

No one tried to tell me to leave.

I think they thought about it but then thought better.

I didn't sleep. The light through the window changed from sun to shadows. I didn't know how many times. Once? More? I didn't care.

Nurses and doctors came in and out. They talked. I didn't listen.

His hand was cold, all the time.

I didn't eat.

Sadie and Vance came by after dark. They tried to talk to me and be encouraging. I listened to them a little more than the others, but not by much. I said nothing. Sadie came back on her own at one point, but she didn't talk at all this time. She just sat with me.

Sam came by. I felt her hand on my shoulder, then my hair. She didn't speak, and I was grateful.

Time passed. I know it did. The light kept changing.

《○》

"There's been more attacks."

A voice came from the door. I didn't recognize it at first. Blinking was difficult because my eyes were so dry as I lifted my bleary gaze.

"Who the hell let you in?" I mumbled.

"I'm too charming to say no to." Parker flashed that gleaming smile at me. I would have groaned or snorted if I'd had the energy to give a damn. The smile faded as he stared at me longer, and I thought I saw...maybe compassion? At least, I saw the smart-ass leave. "There have been more attacks."

"So?" I drawled, looking back at my brother and resting my forehead against his hand.

"That thing is still out there, and she's hurting people." He said this like I didn't understand what "more attacks" meant.

I sighed heavily. "You're a hunter; go hunt it."

The silence that followed carried on so long, I began to wonder if he wasn't there anymore. I looked up, but he was. His lips were twisted like he'd sucked on a lemon. "I can't."

I stared at him.

"I can't," he repeated, louder. "I'm trying, but...I don't have your animal side."

"Was that supposed to be a joke?"

He snorted, looking downright petulant now. "I'd be a happier person if it was, but the truth is, this thing... It's just fucked up. My usual tricks don't work, and I don't get into the mind of an animal like you do. Someone needs to catch her, and I'm beginning to think you're the only one who can."

I put my head back on my brother's hand. "I can't."

"What?"

"I can't."

"Come on, after what I just a—"

My head jerked up. "Get out!" I shouted. "*Get out!*"

He actually flinched, then left.

More time passed, but I didn't care. I couldn't leave my brother. I just couldn't. He had to be okay, he just had to be. I couldn't even process the idea that he might...

☾O☽

"Dakota."

I jerked awake, startled. Apparently, I'd fallen asleep.

Sam was kneeling beside my chair. "You don't want to hear what I'm going to say, but you need to get back out there."

"No."

"Dakota," she said, then paused and lowered her voice. "Anneliese."

The sound of my childhood name made my body tense. Sam was one of the few who knew, one of the few I'd trusted that much. The tension passed, and I felt like I would cry. I clenched my teeth.

"Anneliese," she repeated, knowing the impact of that name, "that thing attacked the wolf pack, the whole wolf pack, during their midnight run. She put two little kids in intensive care."

"I..." I started, but I faltered. *Kids.* I looked at her and then back at my brother.

"Come with me," she said, taking my hands in hers. I didn't know why, but I let her pull me to my feet and into the quiet of the corridor. "You have to catch this thing."

I swallowed hard and winced. "I can't, Sam," I said, sounding like I was pleading. The fact that I didn't hate hearing the sound worried me. "I can't!"

She stared into my eyes. "You *have* to. You're the only one—"

It was the words "only one" that triggered me.

"Don't you get it?! He is the *only* family I have left!" I forced the words through gritted fangs that my emotions decided to create on their own. "I used to have a mother, and a father, and five—*five!*—brothers and sisters. I watched my mother get bludgeoned to death for daring to protect her children. I watched my father and three of my siblings carted off to be burned alive, just for being what we were. Then I had to help kill my sister because I learned her soul was evil. Now, he is the only family I still have! I can't leave him, like I had to leave the others! I can't lose him!"

Even with my raging and my hands gripping the front of her shirt as we stood in the empty hospital corridor, those beautiful gray-green eyes held my gaze without fear and without flinching. She lifted her hands and took my face between them. "No," she whispered, "he's not. I have seen the people around you. You have a new family." Her touch and her words sent an electric shock through me. "And he will be okay, even if we have to drag him back from the edge of Hell ourselves." The plural did not go unnoticed by me. Her hands moved in the blink of an eye around my shoulders, pulling me into a kiss—brief but firm—before breaking off and embracing me. I stood frozen with shock for a moment before I moved my arms around her waist and all but crushed her against my body.

After several long moments, she pulled back to look at me again.

"But right now? He would want you to protect people. He would want you to go out and hunt this thing down and take her out, so she can't hurt anyone else." She smirked a little. "And after this is over, we need to talk."

I held her gaze again and felt an ache deep in my heart. I missed her.

I loved her.

This time, I kissed her. I slammed her back into the wall and captured her mouth with mine, searing both our souls.

Then I tore myself away and stormed down the hall to the doors. She was right. I had to take this thing out before she hurt, or even killed, someone else's family.

☾ O ☽

"There's some kind of pattern," Parker said.

There was a paper map spread out on the hood of his car. It was one of those big, classic muscle cars. (I wasn't surprised.) He pointed to where he'd drawn red circles around different locations in Adelheid. He was right. There was something there. I couldn't say I thought it was a pattern, precisely, but there was something to it. Something that I couldn't put my finger to...

"You said you don't have my animal sense," I said while looking at the map. I traced the points with one hand, and in the other, I had a double-meat sandwich. I'd kept vigil over my brother with neither food nor sleep for four days. If I was going to hunt anything, I would need fuel. "So what *do* you have?" I asked around a mouthful. I had no manners, but I didn't really think he'd care.

"Don't splash me with holy water if I tell you, alright?" he said.

"Demon?" I asked, narrowing my eyes. I smelled deeply. "Alternative plane kind, right?"

He chuckled and shook his head. "You are good."

"No sulfur," I explained simply. "What abilities, then?"

"I can sense energy trails like you pick up on smells," he explained. "By the way, you have the loudest energy of any creature I've ever known. That's saying something."

He had said that before. I wasn't sure how to take it then and I still wasn't sure how to take it, but I couldn't really worry that much about it at that moment. There were more important things on my mind. "What happens with this one?"

We both leaned back against the hood. I ate and he talked. "I guess it's like with your scent tracing. I'll pick it up for a while and then it vanishes when she does her hop, skip, and jumping thing. Teleporting, you said?"

"Yes." I rolled my eyes. "Pre-Tech was doing some really, really dumb-ass things."

"Created a person-cat who teleports, maybe more, and seems to have embraced their darker human side and the hungry animal side together?" he said. "I would call that dumb-ass, yeah. If I was being generous, and I'm not feeling too generous."

Emotion burned a hole right through my center as I thought about my brother. "Yeah, I'm not feeling too generous either."

I finished my sandwich, and we turned back to the map. Parker went around to get something off the passenger seat of his car. "Your cop girlfriend gave me this."

My brows knit, and I considered asking why he thought…how he knew…but he looked at me and gave me a very clear 'do I look like an idiot' expression. I remembered his comment at the reception about hearts and didn't ask. "You two have energy trails that mesh when you're together," he answered the question I didn't ask. Then he added, "You've got good taste, at least," he said instead and brought the file out. "While you were out of commission—" I appreciated that he was at least a little kind there. "—I found a couple of the people in this file. They talked once they knew I wasn't a cop. It didn't really take much pushing, because it seems even the criminal types in the area didn't like this JJ woman too much."

"Alright, so what did they say?"

"She had a hell of a temper and didn't let anyone off the hook. If she felt slighted, she would go for someone. I think that's why she killed that one, the one you found, because she was another dealer who tried to move into JJ's turf. She was stupidly territorial," he went on. "I think that accounts for a lot of the other attacks. This was her area, and she's defending it. A human drug dealer and a big cat, who are usually known for their territoriality, in one body..." He waved his hand at the map. "Most of these are still in that territory, but there's..." His brow knit, like he was trying to solve a puzzle. "There's...movement. Like she's shifting, no pun intended."

"Movement..." I repeated the word thoughtfully, feeling like that meant something I should know. I looked over his little red circles again. It felt a little like looking at a swarm of bees in a cartoon that were about to form a shape, like an arrow, but what was the arrow pointing to?

"You *know* something..." He was staring hard at me.

"Oh my god," I whispered. I realized what the arrow was pointing to. "I know where she—"

My phone rang. I grabbed it and looked at the number.

Lorelei.

I answered. Amid the barking dogs, all I heard was, "—t's here!"

All the oxygen left my body. I didn't say anything, just took off running. Parker shouted after me, but I couldn't have spoken even if I had been inclined to. I ran as hard as I could until I was able to take to the sky. Panic made my flight erratic, but I didn't lose the air currents. I flew as hard and as fast as I could, even though this form was not my best. I had to get there fast. I had to get there in time.

The dogs were all going insane by the time I reached the house. I could see some were loose, but I didn't have time to do anything about it. I landed and found the front door beaten down, shredded. Dishes were broken all over the kitchen floor, and blood was scattered on everything from where someone had stepped on them. I heard growling and the breaking of furniture down the hall. Instinctually, I raced after the noise.

Buster was barking on the other side of my door as the jaguar banged against it, half-human and half-cat. I didn't know where Lorelei was, but I just prayed she was okay. I reached for my tranquilizer gun and quickly cursed because I didn't have it. Did I leave it with Parker in my haste, or was it still in my car? It didn't matter; I didn't have it. That meant that I was entirely on my own here. Just me and a plethora of animal forms.

I ran down the corridor with the speed of a fucking freight train, because that's precisely what I needed to be. By the time I hit her, I had picked my brother's favorite form: bear, although black bear and not grizzly because getting stuck in the hall would be a bad thing.

My weight drove her back as we collided together into the far wall, smashing the mirror off its hanger and shattering it beneath us. I pinned the freak beneath me and smacked my claw across her face. She roared and then screamed something that sounded distinctly human as I knocked one of her fangs clear out of her mouth. She thrashed her head from side to side in pain, and I smacked her again before snapping at her neck.

Instead, I collapsed and smacked into the floor as she ported out from under me. If my ursine mouth could have formed the sound, I would have cursed. Instead, I growled and pushed myself up, turning my large form in the tight confines of the hall. Just as I did, I had a feline face-hugger. She launched herself at me and wrapped her body around my head. I felt the curved claws digging into the back of my head and my neck, drawing blood and sending lancing pain to every corner of my body. I tried to make some kind of noise, but too much fur was in my mouth and nose. If I wasn't fast about this, she might well suffocate me.

Swinging my upper body from side to side, I smacked her into each wall. A loud thudding noise filled the house as I did so, my weight behind hers. With each one, however, her claws dug in harder and the pain increased. So I swung harder and hit harder. She hissed with each collision until she finally jumped off me, turning and running deeper into the house. Shifting again, I pursued. A bear doesn't get a lot of speed in your average New England farmhouse.

However, cats aren't always good at corners. I slid and skidded into the wall trying to haul myself around into the living room. I couldn't gain purchase in the hardwood before I was already careening down. The bitch was on me again before I could take back a bigger form and handle the collision more easily. We fell in a ball of fur and claws. I was not feeling as strong as I usually did, and the crack to my spine as I landed back-first hurt like hell. For a moment, I almost worried that I'd paralyzed myself, but all my limbs were working as I fought against her.

Somewhere down the hall, a door slammed into the wall. I heard claws on the wood floor but didn't know what was happening until I saw a blur leap into the air and land on the jaguar's back. It was Buster!

I wanted to shout at him to get off her, that I didn't want him to get hurt, but I couldn't. The bitch reared back, swinging her arm like she was swatting away a fly. Without a good grip, she managed to smack him off her back and send him flying into the wall with a yelp. Still upright, with her bottom half keeping me pinned, she screamed and bled and I knew Buster must have at least gotten a chunk of her.

"Dakota, stay down!" I heard Lorelei yell.

I tilted my head to look behind me and saw her standing there with a big-ass hunting rifle that I hadn't even known she owned. I heard the concussion and saw the flash of the muzzle blast as she fired without hesitation. The human-animal mix above me jerked like I've seen bodies do in movies as the bullet hit her shoulder. Then her head snapped back when another one struck straight between her eyes, and a small shower of blood rained down on me.

She fell back off me and landed hard on the floor. I shifted to human, scrambling out from under her as I wheezed and got to my feet. Neither of us said anything as I rushed to Buster, who was trying to get on his feet and come to me. I picked him up, which made him whimper again.

"I'm sorry," I whispered.

"My truck!" Lorelei said, and I hurried out after her.

She drove like a bat out of hell. I held Buster while I dug my cell from my pocket but found I couldn't use it around his large form. I dialed Sam but handed the phone to Lorelei. She looked confused for a moment until she saw the number on the display. When Sam answered, Lorelei explained the situation. I could hear her even without speakerphone. Parker had already called the cops, and they were on their way.

I love you, Sam, I thought.

CHAPTER TWELVE

Lorelei and I sat tensely in the exam room of the emergency vet while they took Buster away for an x-ray.

"I'm sorry," I mumbled without looking at her.

I felt her gaze on me. "What?"

Wincing, I forced myself to speak louder. "I'm sorry," I repeated. "For what I did to you at the hospital."

"I'm sorry for what I said," she said in a similar mumble. "The hospital let me in anyways, while you were asleep."

Finally, I turned to look at her. She smiled. I smiled. "Tell your lover to marry you so your sister-in-law can't be such a bitch again, okay?"

I swore I could see a blush on her dark skin.

"I don't like the danger he puts himself in when he helps you," she went on, but didn't look at me as she said it. "But I also do know he's an adult. He has to make his own choices. I know he's your brother, and you would put yourself in front of a bullet for him if you had to."

"I would for you too," I said quietly. "You mean too much to him. And it's been a while since I had a sister." I swallowed hard. "I would for you too."

She looked at me with her brows up and eyes slightly widened.

Before either of us could get deeper into the embarrassing heart-to-heart, the door opened with the vet and the vet tech carrying my dog. I leaped up so fast that I almost fell back over, hurrying to the table as they set Buster in his cast down.

"A broken bone in his leg and a dislocated joint in his shoulder, but he'll be fine. Keep him quiet—"

"All he does is sleep anyway."

"—and we will give you some painkillers for a while as he heals."

I smiled. "Thank you," I said, leaning over the table and gently hugging Buster. He leaned his square head against my shoulder like he was telling me that everything was going to be okay. I could just about believe him, even though he didn't say a word.

☾ O ☽

"Don't you know watching the news is bad for your health?" I asked with a smirk as I walked into Edward's hospital room.

Two days after my 'run-in' at the house, my brother's preternatural healing had won out and he had woken up. Lorelei and I had been there, and we both cried. Yes, I fucking cried. I hadn't cried since I... Well, since I helped kill our sister. This time, at least it was a happier occasion.

That was a week prior, and now he was getting out.

While he was in the hospital, Lorelei and I continued patching things up—between ourselves and in the house. We found all the dogs. As Lorelei put it, it's handy having a hunter for a sister, and I refused to tell her how squishy her calling me her sister made be feel. Everything was put back the way it was meant to be.

"Following the events in the city of Adelheid, Pre-Tech is under investigation—" the anchorwoman was saying as I lifted my head to look at the TV. I grabbed his remote and turned it off.

"Hopefully, they'll get the shit they deserve," was all I said before turning back to him.

He smiled. "I'm sure they will," he said. "I'm just glad to be going home."

Lorelei was in the chair beside him, while I sat at the foot of the bed. "To the mess, and the chaos, and the insanity that has become our daily life?" I asked with some amusement. "I mean, we fixed the holes and all, but they all still bark like fucking idiots most of the time."

"I'll be happy to be home," he repeated. "It's my life and I want it back. Hospitals suck."

We brought him home, and he was back to his usual self in no time at all. Once it caught up, the preternatural healing caught up good. And I was happy. No, I didn't think it'd last, because I'm me, but at least for that moment, I was happy.

☾O☽

Parker left town without another word, which also pleased me.

It left me with one final piece of business, and that was what found me walking through the woods with Buster and Sam. He was watching a butterfly like he wanted to catch it but couldn't because of the cast, while I spent most of my attention on her.

"Where do we go from here?" Too much had been happening with the house, and my brother, and all the rest for us to have this talk. Now we needed to, and she was the one to ask the question.

"Where do you want it to go?" I asked. These talks weren't what I was best at. "As I recall, you did the breaking up. I think that makes this your lead."

She laughed softly. "I always did love the fact that you were so straightforward," she said. "I guess I want to try again. I'm not entirely sure why I ended it the first time, to be honest. I guess I just got kinda stupid for a while."

I shrugged. "I'm pretty sure it was my fault. It usually is."

Stopping and turning toward me, I stopped and turned toward her as well. "Start new?"

"Yeah," I said, eloquent as always. I started to lean closer to her, to kiss her, when…

…Buster's leash caught my knees and even my preternatural reflexes couldn't save me from falling on my ass. My leg flew out, taking Sam down with me as well, so that by the end, we were in a pile on the ground with a dog (totally unapologetic) licking our faces. Sam laughed and tried to push him away. "Not the kind of kiss I had in mind," she said.

"Me either," I replied, wanting to be mad at him but finding myself unable. Somehow, I still got the kiss I wanted.

At the end of it all, I came to a conclusion. Being liked *is* overrated. Being *loved* is not.

If you want to know more about the town of Adelheid, the people who live in it, and the lore I chose to use when writing these preternatural species, you can check out my series wiki at wiki.authorkbthorne.com.

ABOUT THE AUTHOR

Born a Connecticut Yankee in nobody's court, K. B. Thorne grew up to brave snow and talk fast.

She started reading when she was three and never looked back, soon frequently falling asleep with a book under her cheek. At eleven, she discovered *Night Mare* by Piers Anthony and entered the world of grown-up fantasy fiction. As you can guess, it was all over from there. She started writing at fourteen, then met vampires as a teenager and the concept for what would become Adelheid (now the Blood Rights Series) was soon born. Mia Darien followed a few years later, and the books were released.

However, K. B. is also a third-generation Trekkie. Somewhere in a vault at Paramount is a very angry letter written by her grandmother when *Star Trek: The Original Series* was cancelled, so sci-fi is in the blood too. Alongside a love of love and an adoration for her first love of epic fantasy.

K. B. Thorne is the evolution of Mia Darien after years of learning and living. She has taken both of those things to become a smarter, better writer with a fresh new face and take on the literary world. Thorne writes the urban fantasy, fantasy and sci-fi, while Sadie Johnston writes the romance.

These days, when she's not desperately trying to find time to write, she works as a freelance editor/cover artist/formatter and happily lives her unconventional life alongside her very own Named Man of the North and their mini-tank. (Who is, you know, their son.)

You can find K. B. at authorkbthorne.com!

OTHER BOOKS
BY K. B. THORNE

Writing as K. B. Thorne
Blood Rights Series

Bad Blood
Blood and Thunder
Blood Moon
Written in Blood
Bloodshot
First Blood
Out for Blood
New Blood
Flesh and Blood

Out for Blood Series
Bones & Blood

Bellator (Anthology)
Good Things (Anthology)
Ashes to Sunrise (Anthology)
The Shape of Tomorrow (Anthology)
Born of Defiance (Anthology)

Writing as Sadie Johnston (Romance)
Beauty
Help Wanted (with Viola Dawn)
Threnody (with Alastair Malone)
Here, Kitty Kitty (Anthology)
Amor Vincit Omnia (Anthology)
Second Chances (Anthology)